SUSPENDED
ANIMATION

SUSPENDED ANIMATION

Six Essays on the
Preservation of Bodily Parts

BY F. GONZALEZ-CRUSSI

Photographs by Rosamond Purcell

A HARVEST ORIGINAL

HARCOURT BRACE & COMPANY

San Diego   New York   London

Library of Congress Cataloging-in-Publication Data
Gonzalez-Crussi, F.
   Suspended animation: six essays on the preservation of
bodily parts/by F. Gonzalez-Crussi; photographs by
Rosamond Purcell.—1st Harvest ed.
       p.   cm.
"A Harvest original."
ISBN 0-15-600231-0
1. Anatomical specimens.   I. Title.
QM151.G66   1995
611'.0075'3—dc20   95-12650

Text was set in Bembo
Designed by Kaelin Chappell
Printed in the United States of America
First edition 1995
A B C D E

CONTENTS

PHOTOGRAPHS

MICROCOSM IN A BOTTLE

As a young intern assigned to the pathology laboratory of a Catholic hospital run by a monastic order, I was ill prepared for some of the routines. The nuns administered the place with exemplary efficiency. At each key post an overseer or coordinator (may the youthful levity of those who said "spy" be forgiven) saw to it that cleanliness, order, punctuality, and systematic avoidance of waste prevail throughout the establishment. Not that the vices that stand in opposition to these virtues held me in their grip, for as a newly arrived immigrant in the United States I was perhaps overly conscious of the need to produce a good impression through meticulous respect of the rules, but I still felt anxious and insecure.

I should explain that in my native Mexico, generations ago, a most painful rift between Church and State had spawned severe laws against religious pageantry outside the temples. Public processions were forbidden;

no one could appear in the street wearing an attire indicative of religious affiliation. In time, mutual rancors abated and the observance of such laws was relaxed, but it is still a rare occasion today that confronts the common citizen with a member of a religious order in the dress of his or her calling, especially an apparel that flaunts radical departures from the fashions of secular life. I put down to inexperience and my unfamiliarity with the effects of dress, the curious fact that I felt embarrassed to the point of suffocation if a nun ever addressed me with the intent of rectifying my mistakes. The sisters went about their tasks quietly and unobtrusively, but my bungling kept throwing me in the way of their efficient routines.

One afternoon, upon the unexpected absence of a regular worker, I was put in charge of describing the gross appearance of the specimens removed at surgery and submitted to the laboratory. This is a daily routine, utterly familiar to pathologists: diseased organs, biopsied tissues, and even inert foreign bodies extracted from the interior of the body must be carefully inspected, weighed, measured, described, and sampled for microscopic examination in the manner most apt to document the existing pathology. The day's allotment of tumors and inflamed viscera had already been arrayed on the counter—spoils of the unending mayhem between scalpel and disease enacted daily in sterile battlefields around the world—when I caught sight of a batch of containers set aside. These were bottles identified as "products of conception" on their respective labels. I assumed this to be one more example of the unswervingly methodical ways of the good sisters: specimens of like character were grouped together to facilitate my task. These specimens were the first I chose to take care of.

"Products of conception" is common medical terminology that, for once, means precisely what it says: if there is reason to believe that a woman has conceived, and subsequently tissue exits her uterus spontaneously (in a Catholic hospital one is not likely to see any but spontaneous abortions), such tissue may reasonably be regarded as the product of the conception. The intervention of a physician may be required when retained remnants cause persistent bleeding and other complications. The surgeon scrapes off the interior of the uterus in the operating room and sends all tissues recovered to the pathology laboratory.

Inside the tight-lidded containers there seemed to be blood clots. My duty was to scan them looking for evidence of placental tissue and, perhaps, an embryo or its parts. I was on the second or third specimen, reciting into the dictating machine the accustomed formula: "The specimen is received wrapped in saline-moistened gauze, and consists of multiple, irregular, crumbling fragments with the appearance of blood clots . . ." when I felt a tug on my arm. Behind me stood the "lab sister," clad in full monastic regalia head to toe, rosary at the belt and emblazoned insignias of her order on the large cloth that fell in front of the bodice; and she looked at me with a reproachful and impatient gaze from thickly bespectacled, cool gray eyes that dominated her gaunt face.

I turned to mush instantly. Mesmerized by her gaze, whose strength seemed as if concentrated by the suppression of all other details in the wimple-framed head; unable to understand her speech, couched in a language still largely unfamiliar to me; I stood still, looking like the personification of the most abject idiocy. She ordered me away from the workbench, availing herself of peremptory gestures and that peculiar increase of volume and pitch with which some people address foreigners, as if convinced that a conceptual impasse can be made to tumble, like the walls of Jericho, by the simple expedient of shouting. I was obscurely conscious that I was at fault, but uncertain as to the nature of the gaffe. Nor could I see the road to atonement when I hesitated between addressing her as mother or sister, and between bowing, curtsying, or kissing her ring with one knee bent to the ground, as I thought the humble always did to those vested with the majesty of the Church.

I withdrew to a respectful distance, as she motioned me to do, and thence understood the cause of her displeasure. Products of conception are not surgical specimens like any others. Bloody, ill-formed, insignificant, and clotlike as they seem to the viewer, they must be treated with special regard: not as cast-off fragments of a perishable body, but as beings potentially capable of independent life and possessed of immortal souls.

Truth to tell, most of the bottles had nothing but blood clots inside. In some, bits of placental tissue could be subsequently identified with the aid of the microscope. But somewhere in those bottles there *could* be a human embryo, a fully formed, albeit incipient, human being, claiming for itself the rightful spiritual dues that the Church magnanimously extends to all its brethren. Therefore a liturgical service was appropriate. And therefore I stayed away, looking contrite, while the lab sister prayed and repeated invocations and sprinkled holy water with a makeshift aspergillum over rows of glass bottles labeled "products of conception."

The lesson was not lost on me. I understood that the pathologist must handle certain surgical specimens that are imbued with greater dignity, compared to others, by virtue of an intrinsic metaphysical status. From then on, I would leave these specimens untouched until after the nun assigned to the laboratory had performed the appropriate rituals. At the time, I was less clear as to the nature of these ministrations, their instrumentality and function. Because in the Catholic creed baptism is indispensable to attain eternal salvation, I realized that the sister baptized the products of conception, and I could only reflect with sadness on the number of immortal souls to whom this benefit is denied. Every day, over half a million conceptuses live beyond the first week and are thus brought to the very threshold of implantation in the maternal womb, but fully one-half are lost. Spontaneous abortion may then occur in 8 percent to 33 percent of pregnancies after implantation, as diagnosed by a sensitive hormonal method (assay of HCG, or human chorionic gonado-tropin), often before the mother is aware of being pregnant. Later, when pregnancy is recognized clinically through physical examination, the incidence of abortion is still 10 percent to 25 percent of all pregnancies.[1]

Whether and when abortuses should be baptized is a ponderous question that used to be hotly debated by theologians. I had an inkling of the nature of their disputes reading the essays of Friar Benito Feijóo y Montenegro (1676–1764), learned Spanish professor of theology and scholar, of the order of Saint Benedict. An unswerving hammering of popular superstitions in Feijóo's writings reveals him as a man of the Enlightenment, and his engaging style as a peerless expositor. His summary of this delicate matter now follows.

Baptism is called for when the embryo first becomes "animated," in the pristine sense of becoming inhabited by an immortal soul. Many have contended that the acquisition of a soul coincides with the time at which movements are first noted, but on this score the authorities have been deeply divided. Feijóo reviews the opinions of the ancients with admirable scholarliness and notes that knowledge of embryology may assist the arduous tasks of theology. It is important to determine at what age the embryo possesses limbs or recognizable parts; for in a tiny, jelly-like amorphous mass it would be well nigh impossible to adumbrate spontaneous motion. Alas, here again the doctors had been at odds with each other. Some said the fetus is well outlined at thirty-two days, others said at fifty, and still others at fifty-nine or more. An ancient Roman tradition, in which it is not difficult to recognize Pythagorean inspiration, claimed that embryonic development proceeds along a harmonious time course that may be reducible to numbers in a series. Thus, semen existed as milk for six days, turned to blood in three more days, became flesh in the following twelve, and this flesh acquired limbs in the next eighteen days. This belief was expressed in a distich:

> *Sex in lacte dies, ter sunt in sanguine terni,*
> *Bis seni carmen, ter seni membra figurant.*

None of these contentions is to be believed, writes Feijóo. Only Hippocrates is credible, who determined that limbs may be discerned in the embryo as early as seven days of gestation if one takes the precaution of immersing the tiny embryonic body in cold water. In a passage that today may make us smile, the friar adopts the stance of a man of the Enlightenment: assent to Hippocrates' embryologic notions is compelled not by respect to received opinion nor by the authority of the Greek physician, but because he alone reported what he actually saw. Hippocrates was also alone in using the experimental method, devising the shock of cold water immersion in order to elicit a reaction. It is true that elsewhere in the Hippocratic corpus he contradicts himself by asserting that limbs are first visible in male embryos at thirty days and in females at forty. But it must be noted, remarks the Benedictine, that this was ascertained by simple inspection, without resorting to the method of cold water immersion.

Motion, now adds Feijóo, cannot be relied upon to diagnose animation. In apoplexy or in syncope, bodily movements are suppressed, yet the body continues to be informed by a soul. Hence there is a probability that the soul tenants the body earlier than is generally surmised. There being such a probability, early abortuses must be baptized regardless of their shape and the presence or absence of visible movements; for it would be an "atrocious tyranny to expose a soul, by denying it this holy sacrament, to forever be deprived of the life of God in the hereafter." Mark that from the moment of conception the embryo never ceases to grow and to be nourished. This must mean that it is actuated by *form* (in the Aristotelian sense of "essence") and what is called "vegetative virtue"; for all that accepts nourishment and vegetates possesses intrinsic *form* with vegetative and nutritive qualities. But we cannot admit that there is in the human fetus any vegetative *form* different from a rational soul, for to do so would be to fall into Aristotle's error. (Feijóo alludes to Aristotle's hypothesis that the human embryo has first a "vegetative soul" and lives like a plant, later a "sensitive soul" and with it the life of an animal, and finally the "rational soul" proper to human beings. The Church condemned as heretical the belief in various subclasses of souls.)

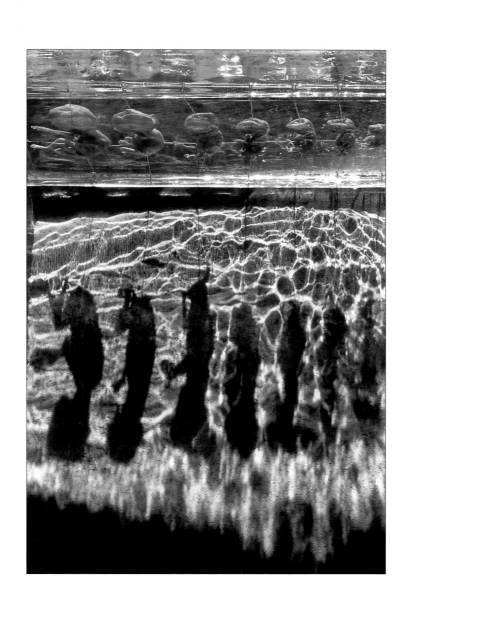

Therefore, the inescapable conclusion is that *human beings possess a rational and immortal soul from the moment of conception.* Feijóo rests his case.[2]

Whatever one may wish to think of theological argumentation, its logic appears more consistent than that of modern legislators. The official status of the unborn, in effect, seems woefully befuddled. In the United Kingdom, an Act of Parliament in 1925 determined that a fetus must be inscribed in the Registry if born at or after twenty-eight weeks of intrauterine life; before this age survival was deemed impossible. Reflecting medical advances in the care of babies, the British Parliament voted on April 25, 1990, to decrease the limit to twenty-four weeks; products of conception before this age are adjudicated "abortuses" and need not be registered as births. But fetuses today may survive if born at twenty-three weeks or less. Suppose twin boys are born at twenty-three weeks, one of them dead, the other alive. The live baby survives, and then, of course, must be registered. His twin, however, is not registered: legally, the surviving baby had a twin brother who was not born! Bureaucratic procedure asks that we erase or disregard reality—an act of faith such as was never asked of us by theologians—and sometimes that we correct it: if a mother delivers a fetus who had actually died weeks before but had been retained inside the womb ("missed abortion"), the dead baby will be deemed a stillbirth and must be registered as such.[3]

Scientific protocols, not metaphysical considerations, enjoin the pathologist to approach the products of conception with delicacy and circumspection. The experts are clear in their admonishments: use sterile saline, not formalin, which brutally hardens structures and alters their color, and close the containers well to avoid dryness. Gently tease the specimen under saline, and view it with a camera-equipped dissecting microscope, ready to photograph the slightest detail. What will you see? Crumbling, crimson-blackish blood clots, in which fibrin threads or bits of endometrium add an iridescent fringe. Often this is all, the products of conception having been previously lost. But patience and perseverance will bring future rewards.

On occasion you will come across a tiny, translucent sac, thin as a grape's skin and full of watery contents. The excitement of anticipation then seizes you: does a homunculus lodge inside? Incise the cover with infinite care, and a viscid fluid oozes out: an embryo is nowhere in sight. Empty, "anembryonic" sacs are not uncommon; either the embryo never formed or it was blighted very early in development and resorbed. Or else the embryo is there, but in a disappointing guise: looking like a tiny, pale nodule in which it is impossible to distinguish front from back, top from bottom—"nodular" embryos are soon aborted—or like a cylinder, up to one-third of an inch tall, in no way reminiscent of a living creature.

Sooner or later, though, the dissector will be rewarded: the bounty of an intact human embryo, at last. Such a specimen begins to be discernible with the naked eye—but it must be "a lynx's eye," according to Feijóo—at about twenty days post-conception, when it measures one millimeter from crown to rump. At this time it has begun to curve, and soon will be C-shaped. Two to four days later it measures two to five millimeters and evinces rudiments of eyes, in the form of little black specks; cardiac activity may be discernible by ultrasonography. At twenty-six days the embryo shows rudiments of upper limbs, which are first like confused protuberances, then like fins. It is doubtful if anyone can prompt it to paddle away, as Hippocrates allegedly succeeded in doing, by immersing it in cold water. In truth, you cannot tell if you are looking at the four-to-five-millimeter embryo of a bird, a mouse, a lizard, or a human: so great is the homogeneity that early life imprints on all creatures. The embryo looks distinctly amphibian. And it has a tail. At thirty to thirty-eight days the finlike limbs show swellings for the hands (hand plates), and it has doubled in size. Elbow regions become recognizable between forty-four and fifty-seven days; at the end of this time toes have sprouted and eyelids are well formed. The entire process of organogenesis is complete by the end of the eighth week. Thenceforth the embryo is no longer an embryo, but a fetus. It lives on, calm and serene in the depths of the mother's womb—"that other world, the truest microcosm" in the words of Sir Thomas Browne.[4] Beneath the vault of its cavern, it is yet encapsulated in a system of membranes or a "chorionic sac," only a restricted area of which develops into the placenta, the complex structure that permits close interdigitation between fetal and maternal tissues.

An odd presence, the placenta, shares the fetal living space. Mark that it, too, is a living presence, since it can develop alone in the absence of an embryo. Little wonder that in many cultures this organ is viewed as the fetus's "double," its shadow or twin brother. Physiologists tell us that the placenta subsumes the functions of all the major organs before birth, thereby lending a certain air of scientific respectability to the wildest contentions of myth and folklore. It functions as a lung, since it establishes gas transfer before the fetus emerges to the ambient air; as an intestine, in absorption of nutrients; as a liver, for metabolism and detoxification; as a kidney, connected with regulation of water and the acid-based balance of the organism; as an endocrine system, in secreting hormones; and so on. As its multifarious protection is plain, the myth-making imagination—Bachelard was fond of saying "the material imagination"—has no trouble seeing a simultaneous power to inflict harm. Consequently it becomes a universal concern to determine the best manner to dispose of this organ once it is expelled.

Anthropologists and ethnographers have yet to compile the entire catalog of local customs for placental disposal. Here it is buried promptly, lest it triggers dreadful plagues; there only after elaborate ceremonies, sometimes under a tree to ensure the fertility of the fields, other times near the homestead to secure the undeviating attachment of the individual to family and country. Or else it must be placed in a pot and washed, as in some rural Thai communities, to protect the baby from skin diseases; or it is placed on a tray bedecked with flowers and floated down the river, at night, to please the crocodiles, as in Java; or thrown into the sea to propitiate a bounteous harvest of fish, as in the Marshall Islands. Scholars surveying over three hundred different cultures found that only seven seemed unconcerned about the manner of disposal of the placenta.[5]

As a pediatric pathologist, I was made uniquely sensitive to the importance of the placenta in the proper interpretation of diseases of infants and fetuses. The autopsy study of a newborn is incomplete without study of the placenta; to attempt postmortem investigation of the lesions of early life in the absence of this organ, those of the trade are wont to say, is like undertaking the postmortem study of an adult in whom the heart or the brain have been left out. However, the industrial West does not share with the rest of the world an elaborate ceremony for disposal of the afterbirth. Accordingly, my colleagues have been known to go to great lengths in order to retrieve placentas from trash bins, incinerators, triturators, coffins, and industrial depots. I have shared this experience. Once, having performed the autopsy of a stillborn that succumbed to a rare viral illness, and aware that study of the placenta could throw light on important but unresolved scientific matters, I was disappointed to find that this organ was not available. I hurried to the clinic in which the birth had taken place only to be told by an attendant of the delivery suite: "The placenta was kept here until this morning. I looked at it, and I can tell you that it was at least twice the normal size, swollen, and discolored." I felt my pulse accelerate. I had a chance to set the entire world's scientific community aright, perhaps to gain immortal fame, once the precious specimen was in my hands. The morgue attendant, however, confused me with the representative of a company interested in producing placental extracts used in cosmetics, who was seeking at the time a supply source. The hospital looked askance at such transactions, and the attendant was laconic. "Well?" I queried, anxious and expectant. "Well," he rejoined, "since it was plainly 'no good,' I threw it out."

Utter unconcern for the ultimate fate of the afterbirth seems to be the rule in industrialized societies. For nearly three thousand years the ancient Egyptians venerated the placenta. An ancient inscription shows a procession in which the Pharaoh walks of a lordly gait preceded by his vassals, while these carry his emblems and most prized possessions, each one hoisted atop a tall staff. One of the attendants displays the ruler's placenta held aloft by its staff, not unlike a king's captain proudly would flaunt a standard with the armorial ensigns of his sovereign.[6] Today, when most births take place in the impersonal, thoroughly technologized setting of a modern hospital, not much is made of magic and myth, and the afterbirth is commonly discarded in the most cavalier fashion. But myth is not about to loosen its powerful grip on our subconscious. The more we vaunt our outwardly rational, scientific attitudes, the more vulnerable we become to our unquenched yearning for the mythical and the magic. How else to explain the odd reactions that the placenta sometimes inspires? An obstetrician of my acquaintance attended a woman during a normal delivery. The father witnessed the birth. No sooner was the placenta placed on a small stand nearby, than the man reached out for it and . . . began eating it! He did not appear to relish the morsel, according to my obstetrician friend, for he retched and vomited copiously after the first few bites.

A gourmet's spoilt sophistication is unlikely to account for this unconventional behavior. Pathologic perversion of the appetite aside, very little support may be summoned for the contention that a mouthful of raw placental parenchyma can be experienced as palatable. I commend the phlegm of the obstetric room's personnel, who apparently maintained an unfazed decorum in the presence of the striking ingestion. After all, they must have thought, in matters of personal taste wisdom consists in the ability to suspend judgment. Yet, the described occurrence cannot be considered exceptional. For in the United States it seems that up to 5 percent of placentas delivered at home are eaten.[7] The "back-to-nature" movement is held responsible for this consumption; "naturists," of course, are likely to deliver at home. Apart from the United States, placentophagy has not yet become widespread in any industrialized society. Although magic potions, ingestible charms, and medicinal porridges are prepared from placentas in various parts of the world, an-thropologists state that prohibitions against placental ingestion are much more commonly reported.

Many animals, as is well-known, regularly eat the placenta. Placento-phagy is so consistently practiced, even by animals that are not regularly carnivorous, that it has come to be regarded as a normal and last stage ("fourth stage") of the process of parturition. It is usually the mother who devours it, and while doing this she seems oblivious of her litter, or of her own needs, since she eats the placenta in preference to customary foods presented to her. Explanations advanced for this behavior include the physiological need to replace nutrients depleted during pregnancy, as well as the uptake of hormones that reside in the placenta, and, when ingested by the mother, stimulate the uterus to contract and the mam-mary glands to function as required for optimal lactation. It is also spec-ulated that prompt disposal of the placenta reduces the chances of attracting predators; apparently, the placenta is left untouched when the offspring is stillborn, since the need to avoid predators is then less urgent.

I suppose advocates of the "back-to-nature" persuasion can draw plenty of arguments from biology and the health sciences to embellish the loathsome practice; placentophagy may yet thrive among the uncrit-ical. But it is likely that fears and anxieties lie at the base of their uncon-ventional ways. Caught up in the life of this century, where nothing but an optimistic profession of faith in the good of science and technology deserves approbation, people are prone to disguise their irrational longings with the cloak of pseudo-scientificism. A striking disparity is much in evidence in the modern world between the stunning, mind-boggling advances in technology and the deepseated ancestral emotions and nonrational attitudes of human beings, which remain fundamentally the same as they have been for thousands of years. Through placentophagy, persons yearning for some form of symbolic expression, but to whom the avenues of ritual, liturgy, and ceremony are forever barred, may have embraced an odd manner to express reverential awe before the incomprehensible, sacred forces of nature.

It is not surprising that the placenta has been perceived by the myth-making, nonrational elements of the mind as the fetus's "double," or its shadow. Both share the same space, and are indissolubly linked to each other by ties of mutual dependence in life and in death. Moored to the placenta by the umbilical cord, like a vessel to the pier, the fetus rocks to and fro, now rising, now falling, ever so slowly, in its watery environment. To the elementary imagination all that is liquid is water, and it is fitting that the embryo and fetus be suspended in this milieu, itself the seedbed of life. Two thousand years ago Thales recognized water as the reservoir of all potentialities of existence; Christian writers, like Tertullian, saw in it "the seat of the divine Spirit," since to it alone among all primeval substances was given the order to produce living creatures. Earth is solidity, the abutment for our bodies and the seat of our sustenance; air is immateriality and indefinite expansion; fire is pure energy, approaching us as welcome light and warmth, or as wind-driven, hissing devastation. But only water is cradle. Only water can impart that total, warm caress that lulled us all into the hypnotic trance of prenatal life, where no thoughts of finitude and decay, no pangs of contradiction and want intrude in the consciousness.

Yet the sign of water is both positive and negative. Life is bodied forth from water, but water can kill. The symbolism of baptism implies submersion into the life-giving waters of the sacred. It is regeneration through rebirth, but in order to be reborn one must die first: the old self dies, and the new self emerges to life. Water is at one time cradle and tomb.

Nothing symbolizes better the bivalence of nature than those bottles containing the products of conception, which one sees in pathology laboratories or in collections of natural history museums. The fetus is there suspended in a liquid, but this liquid is not the cleansing, vivifying water of its original existence: it is a fixative to preserve its structure in death. The membranes of the chorionic sac screen the developing being from noxious influences, but pathologic specimens tell us that sometimes they tear, and their torn strands float waving in the amniotic fluid, encircle the fetus, constrict its limbs, and may amputate its parts. The umbilical cord conveys the nourishment to the fetus as it rocks voluptuously, languorously, in the bosom of its mother. But look at this specimen in a jar: in its listless wanderings the fetus has looped the cord about its neck, and fashioned a constricting figure eight that squeezed out its lightless existence forever. About 3 percent of perinatal deaths are due to loopings, torsions, twistings, and other accidental entanglements. Did a maleficent deity think of both the protection and the danger? This proposition is discussed by Leibniz in his *Theodicy:*

> To deprive a man of his life by giving him a silk rope knowing that he will use it to strangle himself, is as much a murder as to stab him ourselves, directly or through paid assassins. One does not will his death any less in using the first means than the two others: it seems, rather, that one wills it with greater malevolence, since he is left with both the fault and the reproof for his perdition.[8]

The subtle philosopher concludes that this reasoning cannot apply to the workings of the Creator, but all his casuistry leaves us still doubting.

Popular accounts of conception and embryo-fetal development easily lapse into rapturous odes to the invincible powers of nature. Conception is often celebrated in anacreontic stanzas where all is mirth and hope and rejoicing. It is well that this be so, for in the embrace of lovers about to become parents there is something like an obscure, formless yet insistent promise of immortality, so that Diotima could define man-woman love, in the *Symposium,* as "love of immortality." Eternity seems at hand. And when conception occurs, at the very instant of its realization when the flame of a new life is kindled, it seems as if countless sublime possibilities were suddenly mobilized, and the speed of the wheel of time accelerated. When the bottles of champagne are uncorked to salute an infant's birth, who will dare tell the celebrants that on the topmost froth of their drink there is the flavor of death? Who will tell them that the nectar of life comes dashed with flecks of death?

Perhaps no one has to say this. Each one, in due course, will come to realize the life-death bivalence of human existence. The lover who feels transfigured by the power of love salutes in himself "a new man," yet mourns the death of his former self. The parents who exult at the life of their child are thereby reminded of the passage of time and handed an obscure premonition that a new generation approaches, like a tidal wave, to replace them. The mother who senses a new life stir in her womb also experiences dramatic changes in her entire body, and with them a heightened sense of the precariousness and fragility of life. The scientist who scrutinizes the development of new life knows it for an incredibly complex welter of permutations, combinations, chemical reactions and exchanges that must take place in an exquisitely orchestrated fashion. No trials are allowed: genes must be activated at exactly the right time, enzymes released as preordained, and all this under perpetually changing conditions. The slightest misstep, the most trivial omission, asynchrony, or incorrect performance, and the price is death.

Nothing in conception and birth speaks to us about death, yet all in conception and birth speaks to us about death. The products of conception symbolize life's eclosion, its fruitfulness and unflagging, victorious increase. Yet the products of conception symbolize fruitlessness, shriveling, ashes, and death. Nothing in hope, life, love, and the future expresses death. Yet all in hope, life, love, and the future proclaims death and nothing but death. I could conclude that, as in the American saying, the same glass is half full or half empty depending on whether the viewer is an optimist or a pessimist. Or I could invoke the Spanish verse:

> *Todo es según el color*
> *Del cristal con que se mira,*

claiming that "things take the same color as the viewer's colored glasses." However, these metaphors would be inadequate because they imply that the expressions of nature are univocal, and the message is distorted by the interpreter. But I do not believe that the message of nature is one, which is made to sound gladdening when read by Doctor Pangloss and ominous when the scholiast is Doctor Gloom-and-Doom. Rather, the texts of nature are double, like writings that may be read right-to-left or left-to-right, and each reading delivers a different and contrary meaning. Neither palindromes, in which the sentences read the same backward and forward, nor single texts that can be made subservient to the temperament of the reader, but twin texts, each as forceful and impressive as the other—and both equally truthful. We read the one most frequently, because we find it soothing; the other brings no solace, but may be read in many objects around us. I spotted it in saline-filled bottles labeled "products of conception."

OF FLAYING,
DISMEMBERMENT, AND
OTHER INCONVENIENCES

To go from my hotel in Madrid to the medical school at the Complutense University, I must take the subway. My stop, Ciudad Universitaria, is near the end of the line. As the car in which I travel nears my destination, the predominant passenger population becomes gradually more sprightly, garrulous, and blithe. The cheer of laughter, the radiant and jocund smiles, the look of proud energy as it holds open the door of the future: it is the same with young students the world over. The lavish way morning glory has been shed on their cheeks smacks, I think, of arrant insolence. There is no sense in remembering that I was young once. Longfellow had it right:

> From its consecrated cerements
> I will not drag this sacred dust again,
> Only to give me pain . . .

The doors of the car open, and with a throng of youthful faces around me, I make for the exit. It is not difficult to locate the medical school aboveground. I have an appointment to see Doctor Javier Puerta, chairman of the Department of Morphological Sciences, comprising anatomy, histology, and embryology, who will allow me to see the museum of his department: a collection of specimens, some natural, some artificial, used for teaching medical students and physicians throughout the venerable school's long history.

As I have arrived early, I linger for a while in the gray, drab, undistinguished, and outright depressing corridors. Faculty and students come and go. Here, a couple of workers in blue coats trundle an old-fashioned slide projector; there, a teaching assistant hauls a complete articulated skeleton on a stand. Everywhere students come and go, looking as intent as they seem harried by comparison with the subway crowd. In spite of myself, I cannot help wondering whether the instruction imparted in this building is responsible for squeezing the student body dry of its natural glee. For the teaching of anatomy used to be, up to the middle of the twentieth century, and after the abolition of hazing, a kind of sadistic initiation ceremony with official sanction.

Professors figured it was their duty to cram into the student's mind a mass of descriptive data so huge that anyone could see it greatly exceeded the capacity of the container. In traditional anatomical teaching, nimiety and obsessive-compulsive attention to detail were the norm. That an

exquisitely detailed knowledge of anatomical minutia is not really necessary for medical, or even surgical, practice troubled no one. Professors were actuated by the two oldest forces of academia: the invincible inertia of received opinion and the uncharitable solace that comes from seeing others repine under the same wrongs we suffered ourselves. Students, then for the most part unempowered, were too ignorant to appreciate the irrelevance of the curriculum, or, if they aspired to become mentors, consoled themselves by waiting for the day when they could inflict the like torture.

Bones, even the simplest, have grooves, furrows, facets, notches, ridges, and sundry anfractuosities. Each of these accidents bears a name, oftentimes an eponymic name to honor the anatomist who "discovered" it: the foramina of Scarpa, the canal of Stenson, the antrum of Highmore . . . Around the skeleton, soft parts array themselves in astonishingly intricate patterns that the baroque era denoted with understandably hyperbolic gusto: "marvel of marvels," "image of the universe," or "compendium of the vast world." This extraordinary *fabrica* conforms an animated world strapped with flesh and traversed in all directions by pipes, strings and ramifying cords, and conduits, which, down to the smallest branches, must have a name. Muscles, viscera, solid organs, caverns, and recesses: every constituent of the stupefyingly complex system has been given a name. One after another, generation after generation, anatomists were plodding dissectors as well as tireless baptizers. And the names they chose, though a bit unwieldy, lack not a certain hieratic majesty and an aura of mystery—deliberate, no doubt—wherefore they resound like incantations uttered in a cryptic language: *indusium griseum . . . stria medullaris . . . epiploon . . . sternocleidomastoid . . .*

It is quite fitting that dissectors should have been fanatic name givers. For the act of naming is the truest effort to make sense of the chaotic world of sense perception. By naming, we distinguish, arrange, and distribute into categories. How, if not with words, could we handle the overwhelming spectacle that the world presents us at every instant? Trillions of concrete, individual things surround us, but names are always general. With words, as with magic wands, we abstract the general properties of things and avoid turning mad, since it is impossible for each individual object to have a particular and distinct name. To laud the generalization of naming, Leibniz enjoined us to imagine a beach in which "every grain of sand, in short, every grain of sand in the world, must have a [distinct and specific] name." The Leibnizean nightmare is brought home to the anatomy student. If, as an old poetic analogy willed it, the human body may be seen as a stately tree soaked in the vivifying sap that runs through it in a serried circuitry of canals, then every branch, every leaf, and every nervure of a leaf carries a name; and the entire terminology of the human tree the hapless student had to learn by rote.

Wondrous to remark, some students ended up mastering it, or nearly so. Their prowess ranks them with the ancient Greek rhapsodes who memorized tens of thousands of verses, or the fabled medieval minstrels who, after hearing long poems for the first time, could recite them flawlessly, forward or backward. Never mind if their critical powers were none the better for the effort: pettiness alone would dare withhold the laurels to these gallant victors, the dedicated students who so strained their retentive memory. Still, today I am deeply moved when I consider their admirable tenacity.

Santiago Ramón y Cajal, the famous neuroanatomist and Nobel Prize laureate, recalled his student days: By the light of a burning lamp, a textbook in one hand and a skull or a vertebra in the other—one might have said a youthful Saint Jerome doing penance in his cave—he toiled assiduously. Shortly before the examination, he and his classmates would give each other a quiz with such bizarre questions as: "Name a part of the skeleton in which it is possible to touch five different bones simultaneously with the tip of a needle." (Answer: the back of the bony floor of the nasal cavity, where parts of the right and left palatine bones, the two palatine extensions of the right and left maxillary bones and the vomer, or midline bone of the nasal septum, all come together.) How anyone could ever be persuaded that this kind of information might have practical utility is beyond me. Nevertheless, Cajal was not blankly condemnatory of these schooling methods; in a fit of questionable wishful thinking, he owned never having met a person of sound judgment in whom this quality was not rooted in a long-exerted, robust memory.

In the United States, the anatomy student has at his or her disposal all the beautifully illustrated textbooks that have been produced, in addition to modern, computerized systems that can display parts, relationships, and nomenclature. Nothing, of course, can substitute for real specimens, to which students have ample access in dissection and laboratory exercises. Should the learner feel the need to keep a bone handy for ready reference, biological supply companies are happy to oblige. A few hundred dollars will buy disarticulated skulls of natural bone, or exact replicas in plastic, from adult, fetal, or geriatric subjects; these may be intact or painted to show muscle insertions with the bones separated along the sutures and held by springs or cut along various planes.

Where comparable resources are not available, the procurement of bones to enhance the learning of osteology used to be part of the romance and lore of student life. Some of it I can still recollect. Word was passed that an obliging grave digger would, for a modest fee, take the seeker after osseous treasure to the land of plenty: a remote part of an old cemetery where abandoned sepulchers were dug out to make place for the new. At midday, in the bright sun, a small party of silent and intimidated youths followed him to an out-of-the-way part of the vast interment grounds. At last, an excavation appeared, flanked by large mounds of upturned earth. There—we had arrived, and the booty was ours for the taking: femurs like cudgels; breastplates like boat keels; and fine metacarpals like beads of a barbarian's necklace; some partly jutting out of the stirred earth and others submerged, like wrecks and flotsam in a frozen sea.

The vivid sense of repugnance upon the contact of the offal with the gloved hand was not purely physical: the bones were calcined by the sun, and less a danger of sullage or infection than a root or a twig freshly plucked from the ground. But our hearts were heavy with the weight of centuries of prohibitions, religious and cultural, against tampering with human mortal remains. However obscurely, we were conscious of these interdictions and knew that many would regard our act as a desecration or a scandal. Consequently, our macabre excursion had the value of a symbolic challenge: we aligned ourselves with the legions of truth; rallied ourselves with the martyrs who, like Servet, had braved untold perils for the sake of knowledge. For the feeling that to handle and scatter the parts of a dead body is an outrage to decency exists in all of us. And the semi-legendary accounts of early anatomists slinking behind the gibbets to study the body of the hanged are only counterpoise to the belief that to leave the corpse of a criminal exposed, rotting, and devoured by predators is a form of postmortem punishment that adds an extra measure of harshness to the execution. In Britain, the punishment for murder became, in 1752, "gibbeting in chains." The corpse of the victim was treated with tar, enclosed in a metallic framework, and thus suspended from a gibbet raised at the scene of the crime or another conspicuous site.[1] The terrifying spectacle of a tarred, half-consumed, partly decayed corpse, oscillating and creaking in its iron cage, could not have failed to profoundly impress the popular imagination. And it seems likely that this horrid practice did not originate merely from a desire for exemplariness, but from a conviction that certain crimes were so despicable, that ignominy and postmortem dismemberment could alone balance the scales of justice, otherwise ill served by the criminal's "mere" death.

After our sacks and boxes were filled, the gruesome cargo was treated by methods that had been handed down for generations: immersed in quicklime, boiled, and finally varnished, that all could handle the specimens without queasiness. Mine ended up in a cardboard box under my bed. The cleaning lady found them there, and thenceforward refused to clean my room; nor did she approach again that area of the apartment without first making the sign of the cross. Her fears may have seemed erratic, but they bubbled up from a primeval, eternal wellspring in the subconscious that all of us share. In ancient Iran, the Zoroastrians maintained that there is not one soul, indivisible, but a multiplicity of souls; and the osseous soul, one among many, was the pithiest. In many Eurasian communities, all the way to Siberia, these beliefs persist.[2] To the Catholic idea of the resurrection of the flesh they oppose the faith in re-ossification as the first step on the road to eternal life. Zoroastrians, it is generally known, practice the exposure of cadavers, but they take good care to fasten them well, that no bone shall be scattered and be found missing on the day of resurrection. As to those of us who descended into the pit in search of a macabre bone harvest, by this very act we affirmed a different, positivistic tenet: that no soul, no immaterial qualities, and no elements of individual personhood inhere to a heap of bones that have been tossed in the earth and desiccated by the sun.

Before I have time to ask if these bizarre student traditions exist in modern Madrid, Doctor Puerta arrives to meet me. He is young, dynamic, handsome in a distinctly Latin way, and promptly addresses me with the pronoun "*tú*." This unexpected familiarity disconcerts me, as my cultural background dictates a stiffer formality between persons who have just met, but in the end I am pleased by the tone of cordiality thus achieved. He tells me that the anatomical museum was founded under King Carlos III, a monarch whose unflattering portrait by Raphael Mengs—long nosed and exuding a distinctly ovine hebetude under a fleecy white peruke—I had seen at the Prado. The bulk of the acquisitions, however, did not come until the early or mid-nineteenth century, and was largely due to Doctor Julián de Velasco, distinguished professor of anatomy and, like so many of his illustrious peers at the time, avid collector of specimens.

According to my host, an old local tradition maintains that the embalmed cadaver of a young lady existed in the early times of the collection. Julián de Velasco, it was said, "mummified the corpse of his own daughter." My interlocutor uses the tone and gestures habitually reserved for passing on information at face value while arrogating to oneself the right to declare it specious. Real or false, such an occurrence would not be entirely out of character with the temper of anatomists of yore. William Harvey, renowned discoverer of the circulation, autopsied the cadavers of his own father and sister, and throughout much of the nineteenth century an unfeeling attitude, akin to callousness, was propounded by foremost medical authorities as indispensable to the optimal practice of the profession.

The anatomical museum of the medical school attained a respectable size by continuous additions. With pride not wholly exempt of misgivings, Doctor Puerta tells me that this museum is listed in tourist guides that purport to describe "the unknown Madrid." These are, presumably, travel guides aimed to visitors grown weary of common attractions and hungry for exotic fare. But, he tells me, the museum is not open to the public; "budgetary constraints," the sempiternal complaint of departmental chairmen, explain its present state of disrepair. My host then takes me to the hall that houses the collection, and I confirm with sadness the shabbiness of its upkeep.

The hall is a large, rectangular enclosure that may be entered through several doors on one of its long sides. Glass cases, each about eight feet tall, are arrayed across the room's major axis at regular intervals, like benches in a cathedral's nave, and the visitor must circulate laterally, bordering the long sides of the rectangle, as if in a cathedral's ambulatory. Only a lambent, pale winter glow filters through the tall, narrow windows that pierce the long wall facing the entrance. An oppressive air of obsolescence and nostalgia reigns here. Glued to one of the showcases is a sign typed in the minuscule font of an ancient typewriter, whose text has been altered by the incorrect punctuation left by generations of flies. It admonishes: "1. Maintain order and decorum. 2. It is forbidden to toss papers about. 3. Do not touch the glass windows."

At each corner of an end wall, like sentries posted on their watch, stands a skeleton in its glass case. The irony is that the two may have stood guard for many hours in their previous existence, for one is a giant, who by sheer size must have qualified as a recruit, and the other a military man. A label succinctly identifies the former as "Skeleton known by the name of The Giant of Extremadura (1880). Preparation of Doctor Velasco."

Its counterpart in the opposite corner somehow deserves a more explicit sign: "Giant skeleton of a French grenadier"—but the Spanish word for "grenadier," *granadero,* has been mistyped as *ganadero,* meaning "cattle rancher"; the missing *r* has been faintly penciled later, leaving the visitor to ponder the occupational hazards of cattle raising, as the sign continues—"His bones contain a large amount of mercury on account of having been subjected during life to prolonged mercurial frictions." My host points out silvery blemishes of irregular contour on the bony surfaces and clarifies the story. The grenadier, it seems, had come to Spain with Napoleon's army of occupation. He braved the wrath of the vanquished and emerged unscathed from their murderous ambushes; but in the arms of a woman he got more than he bargained for. The tiny spirochete of syphilis began sapping his robust frame in its habitual, torpid style. Left to its sluggish ways, this microorganism would have accomplished in years what the guerrillas tried to do in seconds, trusting to daggers and firearms. The officiousness of medical men determined a compromise: the grenadier's undoing, sped up by mercurial therapy, became a matter of months. The proud Frenchman stayed behind as the former conquerors withdrew, and ended up assigned to perpetual watch duty by the art of Doctor Velasco.

What is it that these imposing sentries guard so zealously? As we walk between glass cases I see dusty, faded models of anatomical and pathological specimens in wax, wood, or plaster, some natural, soaking in fixative, others, more resistant, left to stand unprotected. Many are numbered. Numbers 7, 13, 9, and 16 represent fetuses in the throes of complications of birth: with the umbilical cord looped around the neck, the head hyperextended, or the body about to be delivered in breech presentation. The extraordinary realism obtained by wax modeling lends a terrorizing quality to some pieces: a decapitated head of a fetus that had been retained in the womb shows the bleeding, beefy severed surface in all its ghastly detail. This and other specimens made me glad of being alive at a time when medical advances have largely suppressed the brutal carnage formerly annexed to curative efforts.

I catch sight of two models labeled "*despellejados con hojas de parra,*" that is, "flayed men wearing fig leaves," who expose their subcutaneous interiority—windows have been cut in thorax and abdomen—but retain enough modesty to veil their sexual parts. One is lifting an arm until his hand is level with the top of his head. This gesture is intended to show to advantage the play of the regional muscles during abduction of the upper limb, but it insistently brings to mind the commanding pose of Emperor Trajan's statue. The strange taste of anatomist-curators of yore might well be worth a serious research effort. Skeletons were often arrayed in dramatic poses, like those of orators declaiming or actors performing on the stage. Severed limbs were clad in sleeves fringed with lace, and the most loathsome specimens presented with an eye for the quaint or the picturesque.

The ostensible purpose of these models is to inform. They were intended to teach the medical student the intimate organization of muscles, ligaments, and viscera. Some were cartographic plans or scale models for surgeons to trace the complex itinerary of the scalpel; for the movements of the steel blade admit of no hesitation and are always without return. All the more reason to expect that the artwork should have been a flawless imitation of reality, an arch-faithful rendering of its original model. But this is not at all what we see. The artists who executed these pieces seem to have been, for the most part, incapable of curbing the impetuous flights of their respective fancies.

The artistic representation of "flayed men" (Spanish "*despellejados*"; French "*écorchés*"), apparently much in vogue from the sixteenth to the eighteenth centuries, presents us with a paradox. A man has been skinned: the totality of his integument has been dissected away, peeled off to expose the underlying shiny, trembling, sanguineous flesh. Yet, this man poses in a collected or elegant attitude. He should be lying inert, dead, or else agonizing, howling in the atrocious pain produced by a torture more sadistic than is conceivable. Nevertheless he sits with his legs crossed, reposes nonchalantly against a pillar, meditates, smokes a pipe, or reads a book.

Strange, indeed, was this artistic fashion. In the famous illustrations of Andreas Vesalius's masterpiece, *De Humani Corporis Fabrica* (On the Structure of the Human Body), which some attribute at least partly to the hand of Titian, skeletons disport themselves with cavalier abandon. Leaning its elbows on a tombstone, a skeleton holds a skull in one hand, like a fleshless Hamlet in the graveyard scene, and contemplates it in deep meditation. The skeleton, theme of innumerable "Vanities"—paintings inciting the viewer to reflect on the transitoriness of earthly existence—becomes both subject and object at the same time, as if by some enigmatic circular movement, death was made to meditate on death.

Whence comes the strangeness, the feeling of being sunk in a dream, when these representations were meant to inspire precisely the opposite sentiment, the cool, detached observation of faithfully reproduced reality? Roger Caillois, in an elegant dissertation on the art of the fantastic, notes with sagacity that art succeeds best in achieving a dreamlike effect when it stays close to the perceptions of normal, waking life and that an effect of deep mystery is likelier to be obtained without straying too far from the observations proper to normal, everyday life.[3] Thus, the depiction of a science-fiction monster or the mythological chimera—with its lion's head, goat's feet, and winged torso—may intrigue, astonish, or amuse us, but rarely will it stir the depth of our subconscious in a forceful, troubling way, as only the grandest achievements of fantastic art succeed in doing. Caillois believes the "flayed men" of the baroque period belong to the latter category. They appear to be more than simple bizarre constructs of a feverish imagination: they are beings "who have forgotten to play the role of death." Contrary to our expectations they continue to act as if they were alive; as if the loss of their skin—often the loss of most fleshy parts—were a minor inconvenience, a slight frustration that does not impede their gadding about with charming unconcern. A lithograph from the mid-sixteenth century by Juan de Valverde, one among many of this style, shows a flayed man holding in one hand his own wrinkled skin—in the raw, crumpled, pendulous hide one can see the holes for eyes, nose, and mouth—while in the other he holds the cutting instrument with which, to all appearances, he just skinned himself.

By far the most abundant specimens of the medical school's collection are skulls: two thousand of them, according to Doctor Puerta, who takes his leave while I wander amidst six-shelved glass cases replete with dusty crania. Some are disassembled, others display the bones painted in different colors; there are some from fetuses and infants, but most are from adults. Many are marked with accession numbers and inscriptions across the frontal bone, reminding me of the sugar skulls with the name of a dear friend or close relative that, in Mexico, it is customary to distribute on All Saints' Day. On closer inspection, the inscriptions appear to be notes identifying the skull's provenance: "Ossuary of Ronda," "Ossuary of Almería," and so on. Two thousand skulls! Undoubtedly, Doctor Velasco, the collector, must have been soaked through and through in the phrenological pseudoscience that was fashionable in his day. Had he lived longer, he would have been grievously disappointed. Today, no one believes that the small humps and recesses of the skull's surface mean anything at all, but the learned doctor probably nourished his monomaniac zeal in the conviction that character, temperament, and various mental powers could be read in the conformation of the skull, and that his patient and perseverant hoarding would one day be regarded as a precious legacy to the scientific world. The monotonous spectacle of endless rows of skulls soon tires me. I thank the attendant who holds the keys to the collection, and I go back to my hotel.

On my way back, I reflect on the folly of phrenology. The truth is that the size and shape of the skull are poor indications of the value of its contents: the case does not foretell the jewel, or the stone, inside; some of the finest brains were consigned to paltry encasements. Erasmus, the Dutch genius of the Renaissance, had a skull so small that he was ashamed of being taken for a case of microcephaly. He dissimulated this peculiarity under an oversize beret, without which he was rarely seen in public. This is how he posed for Holbein, and posterity has since been unaware of the humanist's inferior cephalic volume. Voltaire's was also smallish and mean looking: a two-bit villainous roofing, as it were. But under the unprepossessing top, what power! Long after his remains were enshrined with full honors in the Panthéon, the thunderbolts that shot out of his head were still the terror of ignorant bigots. Which is why one of them, a certain du Puymorin, Controller of the Mint, was emboldened to lead the group of fanatical reactionaries who, on an evening of May 1814—thirty-six years after the death of their scourge—penetrated the funeral chamber where the remains reposed and swiped them. The bones must have felt like burning coals to their hands. As soon as they reached a place called Barrière de la Gare, where there was a large refuse dump, they tossed their ignescent load, scattering the bones all around. The skull of Voltaire is no more, but, much to his hateful detractors' annoyance, the wit and charm that hatched inside will abide through the ages with undimmed splendor.[4]

Crowned heads or heads plebeian: once reduced to their bare osseous essentials the distinction matters little. But it is no less true that as osseous boxes their vicissitudes are not over. Take Friedrich von Schiller, the great German literary figure. Death overtook him in Weimar, on May 9, 1805, only three years after he had been ennobled and become *von* Schiller. His coffined remains were deposited in a stately edifice, the Kassengewölbe in Weimar. But the remains of world-renowned intellectuals are not to be casually stocked away and forgotten. Twenty years later, the community saw fit to ceremoniously transfer them to another site, the Fürstengruft. Alas, for this transfer! Eighty years after the poet's death, a monocled professor of archaeology and respected scholar named Welcker looked over the venerated skull, and with due pedantic verbosity detonated a skeptical bombshell: the skull was, in all probability, not Schiller's.

German *Professorismus,* in all its redoubtable power, had been triggered. The anatomist von Froriep took up the investigation. To proceed systematically, it was necessary to investigate the site where the remains were deposited. Only the Kassengewölbe had been demolished. No matter: an excavation was done, and no less than seventy crania turned up. After a painstaking process of elimination, one of these was deemed the poet's skull. The world then saw a succession of German professors agreeing and disagreeing; and all the while, in respective containers, two skulls, one large and one small, posing as putative housings of the illustrious brain. The larger one bears Schiller's name. A few steps away is its

contender, dug out by Froriep. Last in the series of learned examiners was Hildebrandt, whose careful canvassing of the dental anatomy of the bigger skull made him conclude that the latter is, *mit höher Wahrschein-lichkeit*—in all probability—"the real one."

Like Doctor Velasco in Madrid, these German professors might have benefited from Sir Thomas Browne's admonition: "Behold not Death's Heads till thou doest not see them, nor look upon mortifying Objects till thou overlook'st them."[5]

BOLOGNA, THE LEARNED

THE THEATER

I follow my guide in Bologna—*Bologna la dotta,* the learned one, as the natives proudly nicknamed it—with the regret of countless travelers before me: there is so much more here than I can possibly absorb! We turn eastward from a historical section of the city and we come to Piazza Galvani. The selfsame Luigi Galvani, in bronze, bends forward unassumingly atop his plinth. He is that curious gentleman who, in the eighteenth century, first came to the astounding conclusion that electricity is actually generated by living tissues and participates in the normal function of the body. Flanking the memorial that his grateful compatriots raised to his electro-physiological fame, a stately arcade with sandstone columns stretches for over 450 feet. I am told that the elegant of the town have traditionally gathered here for swank, flirtation, and gossip; and it comes as no small surprise to realize that through this portico one gains access to the Palazzo del Archiginnasio, which has been the seat of the university since 1562. Vanity and learning thus adjoin each other, as they ought to in a city with distinctly human features.

Bologna boasts the most ancient European university. Tradition has that it was founded in 1088, although for a long time it was without a fixed seat, and lectures were delivered in various convents and halls throughout the town. The Archiginnasio has only one floor above the portico. On the ground floor there is an elegant courtyard and a chapel with interesting frescoes. I had hoped for a more leisurely survey of the building, but my guide urges me upstairs. I follow sheepishly: this is Italy, where the obsessive-compulsive have been known to be felled by a throbbing confusion of the aesthetic faculty resembling nothing so much as apoplexy.

That this is the Italy of our hearts is further confirmed by the sudden realization that the place we have come punctually to see is closed. Not to worry, though: my guide is a native Bolognese who, without unseemly scrambling, and with barely a thin daub of local color, pleads our cause and obtains redress. The doorkeeper is temporarily out, but the keys have been entrusted to a coworker. The latter presently appears, and the door panels yield to disclose a splendid spectacle for which, as for so many others in this ever-suggestive land, I have come uninformed and unprepared. It is the magnificent Anatomical Cabinet built by Antonio Levanti between 1638 and 1649, and enriched with the work of extraordinary artists and craftsmen.

This gem of a room is built entirely of wood: the eye looks in vain for a place in walls, furnishings, floor, or ceiling that is not covered by elegant woodwork. In the center of the room stands a dissection table with a marble top, girded by a knee-high balustrade. Rising obliquely toward the two lateral walls are steep gradins that make four tiered benches. The back of each bench is a long board that shoots up to chest level for spectators seated on the bench immediately above. It is easy to imagine the eager students of yore leaning their elbows against these barriers, bending forward, keenly absorbed in watching the cadaver dissection below.

The wall opposite the entrance is offered to unobstructed view. One sees here symmetrically disposed niches with statues, also in wood, of famous physicians of times past. Against the very center of this wall is a high seat that, on account of its elaborate ornamentation, could be taken for a king's throne. It is the cathedra, the official chair of the professor who presided over the anatomy demonstration, and it has been placed so distinctly above the observers' benches as to leave no doubt of the lofty academic dignity of its occupant. The thronelike quality of the seat is enhanced by its surmounting baldachin with allegorical figures—the whole in pine and cedar wood—which is supported by two columns in the shape of anatomical figures, like architectural caryatids. These two exquisite figures represent *scorticati,* "flayed men," one placed frontally, the other in profile. They are the work of Ercole Lelli (1702–1766), one of the founders of the Bolognese school of wax sculpture; much of his work was executed at the command of Cardinal Prospero Lambertini (1675–1758), who became pope in 1740 under the name of Benedict XIV.

Cornices, moldings, ornamental bands, tabernacles, benches, and statues are crowned by a remarkable wooden ceiling with a sculpted Phoebus, tutelary god of medicine at its center, and fourteen personified constellations gyrating about him. Alas, this marvel of human industry was turned into a heap of rubble on January 29, 1944, by a bombardment during the Second World War and was painstakingly reconstructed afterward.

The least capacity for appreciation of beauty persuades the viewer that this room is a sample of consummate craftsmanship, but those connected with anatomical dissection will also find it movingly evocative. How was the grave, singular task of cadaver dissection performed here? No fitter place for this musing than Bologna's Archiginnasio: The *Anatomy* of Mondino de' Liuzzi,[1] professor of medicine at Bologna, was written in 1316 and is the oldest "handbook" designed as a companion to anatomical demonstrations.

That dissectors in the Middle Ages risked death and torture to satisfy their intellectual curiosity is apparently a misconception. Cadavers were dissected in twelfth-century Salerno and since 1241 in the Kingdom of Naples. The Church never issued a general condemnation of anatomical learning. True, Pope Boniface VIII, in a bull issued in 1299 and reissued in 1300, threatened to excommunicate those who boiled cadavers to separate the bones from the flesh (a charming expedient used, for instance, when crusaders died while traveling and had arranged that their remains should be shipped back to their birthplace); but prohibitions such as this aimed to curb abuses in the veneration of relics and other misdeeds of a rather spiritual sort. A certain anchoritic contempt for the body inspired many ecclesiastical pronouncements. The soul was all important, and what happened to the decaying husk that had housed it was not the Church's primary concern.[2]

Yet, the occasions on which dissections were actually performed remained few and far between. It is not difficult to understand why. No advance ever occurs in a vacuum, and the body politic must be duly prepared before it can digest, assimilate, and incorporate progress. As to medieval medicine, it is well-known that it could be more properly regarded as a branch of philosophy than a natural science. When medical men wished above all to decide whether the heart, the liver, or the brain "ruled" the body, what relevance could they ascribe to detailed knowledge of anatomical structure? What new understanding could be derived from knowing the disposition of nerves, arteries, and ligaments, when the topic of debate was whether "temperament" could be ascertained by touch, or whether the ultimate "principle" of the body was one or many? Anatomical dissection was uncommonly performed, largely because in the prevailing intellectual climate this method was not expected to shed much light on the questions that most troubled physicians.

Thus, throughout the Middle Ages anatomical dissection was desultory and sporadic. It was sometimes performed in a room of an important person's house at the request of the relatives of the deceased for various motives; sometimes it was done in convents or monasteries, as by nuns or friars seeking objective marks of the holiness of one of their number. What were, I wonder, the anatomical marks of sainthood? Pathologists seem not to have researched the matter. Novelists and poets have, after a manner, but everyone knows that their utterances always pass unheeded. In *Love in the Time of Cholera,* Gabriel García Márquez says that a crystal, refulgent as a diamond, is found inside the hearts of those who commit suicide—for love, of course—by aspirating mercuric compounds used in photographic solutions. We are to understand that only the combination of true love and the chemistry of mercuric crystallization accounts for the strange phenomenon. The rarity of the former explains, I suppose, why I have never come across the coruscating crystal, despite a long acquaintance with autopsies. What is certain is that dissectors see what they want to see, not the organs that their hand displays: no member of the trade, if honest, will quarrel with this statement. Which is why the *medici* opening up the body of a presumed saint would see rubies instead of blood clots and precious gems and lapis lazuli where we—coarser observers that we are—tend to spot gallstones of calcium bilirubinate. Upon the advent of the Renaissance, the things seen became the same for everyone, in the measure that this is humanly possible. Dissection now became an educational exercise: the ascendancy of anatomy, and later of pathologic anatomy, had begun. In 1405 the University of Bologna allowed up to twenty students at the dissection of a male corpse, and up to thirty at a female's.[3] In the following century the demand became so great that amphitheaters had to be built in order to accommodate the audience. In Leiden, the apse of a church, of the former Falie Baginhof, became the Theatrum Anatomicum that functioned from 1593 to 1772. In Padua, at the Palazzo del Bo, the magnificent anatomical amphitheater with its concentric oval tiers was built in 1594 and saw the likes of Galileo and Morgagni deliver lectures. The superb Bolognese amphitheater in the Archiginnasio is another example.

Dissections were public and were widely advertised days ahead. In Bologna, notices were posted on the columns of the Archiginnasio, in Latin, which was the language of the lessons. In Leiden, since anatomical dissection took place in a church, the tolling of a bell summoned the spectators. In Paris, the streets adjoining the School of Medicine were decorated with garlands, flowers, and festoons. Successful physicians, prominent members of the community, intellectuals, and the inevitable idle and rich snobs, apart from medical students, gathered in the amphitheater. This motley crowd generated no small commotion with gossip, bumptiousness, and self-display. Liveried lackeys appeared who circulated amidst the attendees distributing bouquets and oranges to the ladies, that "the perfume of the ones and the sweet aromas of the others" assist them in brooking the unpleasantness of the emanations wafting to their noses from the opened cadaver. Members of the aristocracy received sticks smeared with aromatic resins, which were to be burned during the performance as one more expedient against revolting odors. In Bologna, the front seats were reserved for important officers, the prior, the counsellors and the electors.[4]

The Bolognese amphitheater was magnificently decorated for the occasion: the walls were hung with damask, and two large torches, placed respectively at the head and feet of the cadaver, illuminated the working area. A crimson-gowned professor then appeared, ceremoniously followed by his attendants, and silence descended upon the amphitheater. The prior (whose prerogative it was to interrupt the demonstration at any time by clapping his hands) gave the ceremonial order to begin. The professor used all the ornate erudition of which he was capable to review, in flawless academese, the work of his predecessors; he would then lay out the chief points of the demonstration that was about to unfold.

Between fifteen and twenty topics, that is, organs or systems, were discussed over the course of two weeks. Leaving his gown in the care of an attendant, the professor came down to the table, scalpel in hand, and began the dissection himself. In some cases he would delegate the menial aspects of the work to lesser sorts and expostulate on the significant aspects of the demonstration while indicating certain salient aspects with a long, tapered pointer.

Imagine the scene unfolding: The professor, or one of his attendants, runs the scalpel with unhesitating firmness over the cadaver's chest and abdomen, along the midline. The flesh opens up, exposing wet, glistening, and sanguineous structures behind the blade's long, advancing trail. In the heaviest of silences, the spectators gape at the surface of the viscera that appear when the abdomen is penetrated. The professor sinks a hand in the pelvis, and an unexpected spurt of dark, semiclotted blood stains his shirtsleeve. Not a wink from the demonstrator, but two ladies avert their faces, and the attendant takes a step backward. "Now, now," says the professor reproachfully, "I must have your complete attention. We are not privileged to watch this marvel of Creation every day." He then directs another attendant to remove the intestines by gradually severing the mesenteric insertion with a long knife. With the cutting of the structure that holds them in place, the serpentine bowel loops emerge little by little in a long, straight line, and are placed in a bucket. We are reminded of the gruesome scene portrayed by William Hogarth in his ⌒

famous woodcut, "The Reward of Cruelty"; but, although the spectators have time during the pause afforded by this long procedure to exchange some words, and perhaps some muted, anxious bantering, it is unlikely that they ever resembled the coterie of cynical, uninterested, and raving madmen that Hogarth placed in his amphitheater's background. Meanwhile, in an adjacent chapel, masses are being said for the salvation of the soul of the subject, that is, the person whose cadaver is being dissected.

Once the inner structures were exposed, the lesson could take a rather vivacious and agitated tone. In fact, it could turn chaotic. The long tradition of "academic debates" had survived intact. Scholars raised questions, often sophistical and tendentious, which the professor had to answer. Argument followed counterargument. Opposing factions loudly incited their respective champions. Passions became overheated, and individual glory or opprobrium hung on witty repartee meant to confound the opponent. The dispute became the most important part of the ceremony: the names that decorate the walls of the Bolognese amphitheater—Flaminio Rota, Giambatista Cortesi, and others—celebrate the fame of those who excelled in the difficult art of finding extemporaneous rejoinders to the captious objections.[5] Starting in 1596, admission to the Bolognese demonstrations was made free of charge, thereby allowing the attendance of people who were neither scholars nor members of the trade. We may gather the increased confusion that resulted, since decrees were passed ordering guards to be posted at the doors to discourage the rowdiest and most troublesome spectators. Huge crowds thronged the place when Vesalius demonstrated the anatomy of the female genital system, and eager watchers jostled to get closer to the scene, to touch, indeed, the structures exposed.

It was the same throughout Europe, wherever public anatomical demonstrations took place. Historians tell us of professors in Germany who were compelled to sternly enjoin the spectators, especially during the dissection of female genital organs, to keep due decorum. In Holland, laws were promulgated that tried to check the inappropriate outbursts of persons who laughed, clapped, asked "indecent" questions, grabbed the specimens prepared by the dissector, or otherwise attempted to disrupt the solemnity of the occasion. But it was in Italy, as anyone might have anticipated who is familiar with the warmth, the exuberance, and the superior aesthetic gift of Italians, that the show assumed its flashiest, most striking, and splendiferous features. It is of especial significance that, in Bologna, dissections were performed during Carnival, beginning on the Feast of Saint Anthony (January 17). Accordingly, there was a festive character to the ceremony, and some persons came masked, or in carnivalesque disguise, to watch the proceedings. Yet it was, undoubtedly, a most solemn ceremony; why, with all the politicians, the representatives of the papal power, the prior, the counsellors, the scholars of the university, and the notables of the city gathered under the roof of an ornate and costly amphitheater, there is little question that it was a public performance designed to enhance the academic prestige of the city and to proclaim and reinforce respect for its constituted authorities and established hierarchies.

Public dissections in the amphitheater that I visit, I say to myself, must have been all this, and more. What they were in the *least* measure, apparently, was anatomy lessons. In effect, what could be the instructional value of the demonstration for the hundreds of attendees who did not speak Latin, did not have the requisite background, and could hardly see the organs exposed from their crowded and distant observation posts? At most, they would be entertained by the heated and ingenious *disputatio,* dazzled by all the pomp and ceremony, and, by rather remote chance, morally edified by the spectacle of the body's disintegration. For public dissections had, in addition to all the attributes aforementioned, a moralizing intent. The demonstrators would use every opportunity to point out, in their most eloquent rhetorical style, that the ingenious design of the body was one mark of the infinite goodness and supreme wisdom of a beneficent Creator. Moreover, the mentality of those times was uniquely prone to dwell upon the idea of the body's fragility and the insignificance of our corporeal nature. Art, literature, and popular folklore during the baroque era spawned the *Vanitas,* a whole artistic genre devoted to bring to conscious contemplation the inescapable fact that we are but dust, and that unto dust we shall return. Presumably, the spectacle of a lifeless human body being cut, rent, divided, and consumed, would effectively impress the unholy with the idea of their inexorable end and the immediacy of eternal retribution. Unfortunately, it seems to me that moral reform by visual shock is rarely attained, and I have no reason to suppose that it was otherwise with the jokers who came clad in carnival disguise to watch the demonstrations.

If the professor was not utterly without a sense of humor, he, too, might allow himself a moment of restrained levity. "I wished for a long time," he says, "to demonstrate for you the course and relationships of the inferior vena cava. But, as you know, lately we have been short of *volunteers.*" In a way, these "volunteers" were the central protagonists of the demonstrations. They were, indeed, very difficult to come by. Typically, dissections were performed on the corpses of condemned criminals and, according to law, on "unknown and ignoble bodies . . . from distant regions," whose disassembling could be carried out "without injury to neighbors and relatives." Accordingly, candidates for anatomical dissection were the homeless, foreigners without known relatives, and generally those without the means to ensure a proper funeral. In a word, the poor.

The poor, the marginal members of society, have always been likeliest to become material for pedagogical or investigational anatomical studies. It was so in the past, and remains so today. This sobering phenomenon has been the subject of thoughtful scholarly inquiry and deserves at least a brief comment here. Disease leaves its imprint on our bodies, but diseases afflicting the poor tend to be different from those of the affluent. Malnutrition, parasitic infestations, consumptive illnesses, and infections acquired through neglect and substandard protection are seen with much greater frequency in the poor. Robert Sapolsky, a professor of biology at Stanford University, argues that erroneous concepts derived from studies done almost exclusively on destitute individuals have had untoward consequences for society.[6] He uses the mistaken estimate of the size and weight of the thymus as an example of tragic consequences. The thymus gland is placed inside the thorax, just behind the sternal bone, and is very prominent in healthy infants and young children. However, its size decreases dramatically under conditions of stress in response to the secretion of steroids from the adrenals. That a life of poverty and deprivation is chronically stressful hardly needs reemphasis. Inured to seeing smallish thymuses in autopsy after autopsy, pediatricians mistook the normal thymus for an enlarged or hypertrophic gland and created the high-sounding diagnosis of status thymico-lymphaticus for children who harbored, in reality, a perfectly normal thymus. Sapolsky argues that this mistake would never have happened if autopsies had been regularly performed on patients representing all segments of the population instead of concentrating almost exclusively on those belonging to the lower social strata.

Infants who die suddenly, and who today would be classified as examples of the so-called "sudden infant death syndrome" (SIDS), were

thought between 1925 and 1955 to succumb from an enlarged thymus compressing the trachea and causing a lethal suffocation.[7] With the best of intentions, the medical profession recommended radiation therapy, which effectively reduces the size of the thymus, to prevent the alleged tracheal compression. This was a most unfortunate decision. Status thymico-lymphaticus has the esoteric ring dear to the medical profession; therefore, it was a diagnosis apt to be made whenever a normal thymus showed up on the X rays of a baby. By the time I was a medical student this concept was already obsolete, thus I never saw a patient in whom this diagnosis was made. What I did see was the appearance of cancer of the thyroid or other malignancies in adolescents or young adults who had been subjected to radiotherapy for status thymico-lymphaticus when they were infants. A strong presumption links the ill-advised therapy and the subsequent development of cancer as cause and effect.

The situation regarding autopsies was not much different in the Renaissance: destitute persons without families, strangers passing through town on a pilgrimage, and executed criminals whose crimes made them deserving of opprobrium were likeliest to end up on the dissecting table. Because executions in Italian cities of those times numbered three or four per year, the total number of available corpses was meager. Nor is this all. In the days before the invention of artificial refrigeration, dissections could be performed only during the winter months, usually December to February, and work on each cadaver could last only three or four days.

Much to their regret, anatomists had to work at a very fast pace, skipping those delicate and flimsy structures whose comprehensive delineation would require many hours of meticulous toil. Unseemly behavior was soon sparked by the scarcity of cadavers. In Bologna, complaints of grave robbery by medical students date from the early fifteenth century. *Burking* (a quaint term coined from Burke, an infamous English assassin who sold the bodies of his victims to anatomists for a profit) was still unheard of, but overzealous anatomists were known to snatch a corpse or two when the grief-stricken relatives were distracted, and even to forcibly assault funeral processions.[8]

An obvious remedy to these ills was to devise the means to preserve the structure, color, and texture of the tissues and organs, in all their delicate and complex relations, beyond the time when decomposition sets in. Alas, in the rudimentary state of science at the time, this was more easily said than done. Gallant efforts, however, were not found wanting. Everything was tried, from simply boiling and drying the subject (the "excarnation" method), to tanning it, to soaking it in honey or in wine—the usefulness of alcohol in embalming was well known to Ambroise Paré (1510–1590).[9] Then, two methods were devised: intravascular injection and ceroplasty, the art of modeling anatomical specimens in wax.

Ceroplasty flourished especially in the north of Italy. Some of the wax models produced here reveal such exquisite craftsmanship, and so accomplished a mastery of traditional aesthetic rules, as to leave no doubt that they must be ranked with the most sublime productions of the art of statuary. Why this generally has not been so, has, I believe, two explanations: first, they were intended as adjuncts to anatomical studies, that is, as "teaching aids" for medical specialists; and second, the choice of subject was apt to create in delicate aesthetes or squeamish art critics the sudden urge to go home and consult Ruskin. Indeed, the illustrious precursor of wax modeling in Italy, the mysterious Sicilian Giulio Gaetano Zummo (or Zumbo, as is sometimes written) (1656–1701),[10] chose to represent the process of cadaveric decomposition as one of his major themes: the haunting scenes of his *teatrini,* or "little theaters," entitled "The Plague" and "The Triumph of Time," are sculptural compositions mercilessly strewn with decomposing, putrescent, mottled, or livid corpses in various stages of organic decay. Madame Élisabeth Vigée-Lebrun (1755–1842), outstanding French painter of the ancien régime and portraitist of Marie Antoinette, visited the shop of another wax modeler, the eximious Fontana, in Florence. The Florentine master opened a cabinet to suddenly reveal the extraordinary representation of a recumbent woman with the abdominal cavity exposed and the glistening, humid viscera rendered in shockingly realistic detail. Vigée-Lebrun could not fail to recognize this work for a feat of technical virtuosity and uncommon talent. But for many months after this experience she could not rid herself of the image, and she averred she could not observe attentively any person, or study a sitter for a portrait, without imagining at the same time that the colon, the loops of intestine, and the panoply of ramifying blood vessels that supply them protruded through the abdominal surface and exposed themselves in the identical arrangement she had seen in the statue.[11]

THE WAX MUSEUM

My guide now takes me to the Institute of Anatomy of the School of Medicine in Bologna, where I briefly stop before the superb wax *scorticati* or flayed men of Ercole Lelli, displayed inside handsome eighteenth-century cases. Lelli, whose admirable woodwork we noted at the Archiginnasio, was commissioned by Cardinal Lambertini to produce an entire collection of statues. Beginning with two nude figures, male and female, different stages of dissection all the way down to the skeleton were to be portrayed. The two figures placed at the entrance in respective cases display the external anatomy before the scalpel lifts off the skin; posed together, they cannot fail to remind the viewer of Adam and Eve. The remaining sculptures seemed to me to have retained their elegance beneath a two-and-a-half-centuries-thick patina of almost complete neglect. These figures are life-size and may be said to be lifelike in more than one way: Lelli used real skeletons as the framework upon which the wax-modeled soft parts were superimposed. No less than fifty or sixty cadavers were dissected in order to complete the commissioned work.

Lelli's successor was Giovanni Manzolini (1700–1755), a competent artist whose works are also on display. With the help of his wife, the remarkable Anna Morandi Manzolini (1716–1774), a woman made professor of anatomy by order of the Senate of Bologna, the two executed anatomical works that won the admiration of their contemporaries. Realistic wax busts of this singular couple are still shown at the Institute of Anatomy. After seeing these statues, however, I am disappointed. Everyone is familiar with the uncanny realism of wax models. Artists have exploited it to reproduce the color, the freshness, the appearance of living tissues, or the livor and wanness of death. But here, after centuries of benign neglect, the exhibits have acquired a dusty, faded, and lusterless quality that reminds me of the tawdry itinerant freak shows of a bygone era. And I see none of the truly great productions of wax statuary that I have read about. My guide, a young and pretty medical student, informs me that the pieces I wish to see are kept in Florence. I adopt, nonetheless, an interested outward demeanor as demanded by the most elementary politeness, here reinforced by the comeliness of my hostess; inwardly, however, I resolutely purpose to cut the visit short. Then, to my surprise, I discover a strange object. At one corner of the exhibit hall there is a model of a human fetus that has been placed inside a container that looks like a wineglass. The oddity of this arrangement launches me into daydreams.

Who chose this manner of display? Was it fortuitous that a wineglass was thought fit to take the place of the womb? The ancient Greeks, struck by the role of the uterus as recipient or container of the developing embryo, referred to this organ by terms that modern translators render as "vessel" or "jug." The term seems apposite, considering that the womb does look like a bottle whose neck points downward. However, a distinguished student of Hippocratic texts, L. Dean-Jones,[12] observes that in various sources the word used for the womb is *askos,* a wineskin; and because it is repeatedly described as being soft, pliant, and capable of being distended by the continuous growth of its contents, it is likely that the general image of the womb in ancient Greece was that of a wineskin. But the womb was also supposed to have the ability to draw moisture into its hollow cavity. By what mechanism? A passage from the Hippocratic Corpus quoted by Dean-Jones shows that theories attempting to link anatomical form and function were rife in antiquity: "if you gape with the mouth wide open, you cannot suck up any fluid, but if you pout and compress your lips and insert a tube, you can easily suck up as much as you like." In other words, the generalization was drawn that organs whose shape is wide at one end and narrow at the other are uniquely fit for suctioning blood, moisture, semen, or whatever fluids the Hippocratics deemed conformable to their physiological hypotheses.

The simile is striking and takes us still further afield. Between sucking up fluids with a straw and drawing blood or male seed into the womb, there are more than accidental affinities. In the former case the fluids are impelled into the throat; in the latter, to the female internal genital system, which is a "throat equivalent" to the untutored imagination. In effect, the ancients believed that a kind of sympathy existed between the throat and the womb—"upper and lower throats," says an ironical modern commentator—and that a girl's throat distended when she lost her virginity.[13] I would not wager that we, children of the Technological Era, have rid ourselves of this irrational thought. Galen reported that "Herophilus likens the nature of the uterus to the upper part of the windpipe." Centuries later, Saint Isidore of Seville, last of the great Fathers of the Church, remarked in his *Etymologies* (perhaps the most authoritative reference work throughout the Middle Ages) that women dancers, obese women, or those engaged in strenuous singing competitions fail to menstruate and are infertile, the reason being that nutrients are "consumed" in the effort, instead of allocated to normal use in procreation.[14] The peculiar inclusion of singers among the candidates for infertility points out the multisecular perdurability of the "archetypal" idea, as Jung might have said, of a connection between throat—or larynx—and the generative system.

Well into the nineteenth century, the notion survived. A scholarly book by Thomas Laqueur that looks at the evolution of anatomical concepts influencing our ideas of gender difference reproduces a nineteenth-century anatomical illustration of the inlet of the larynx, viewed from above. The structures portrayed were rendered in as true-to-life a manner as could be expected from a textbook of anatomy. Yet the artist's subconscious must have been prey to the ancestral irrational image: he (or she?—this would be interesting to know) used shading to so exaggerate the relief of certain areas while diminishing others, that the total effect is to make the larynx strikingly like the external female genitals. These true and false vocal cords might pass for labia minora and majora, respectively, complete with a point of convergence in which the observer would almost discern a clitoris, and the structures surrounding the larynx so treated as to inevitably bring to mind the perineum and its major bony landmarks.[15]

The style of this anatomical plate, with its beautiful, laboriously executed line shadings, reminded me of my days as a medical student when it was my unwelcome duty to retain a mass of anatomical data vaster than my weak memory could possibly hold and far greater than the likelihood of my ever putting any of it to useful employment. It was in ponderous volumes full of illustrations such as this one, admirable products of the heyday of biomedical freehand illustration, that I first learned anatomy. Of the huge burden of facts that I had the obligation to consign to memory, few condescended to stay therein. But I still think with delight of the beauty of the illustrations and the liveliness of each chapter's introduction. Curious facts, bits of history and folklore, and brief medical anecdotes were arrayed at the beginning of some sections of the textbook. It was as if the kind authors, conscious of the dreariness they anticipated, wished to regale the student with a little amenity before surrendering to the arms of their habitual, soporific muse. Thus, I still remember, and have since verified—by pulling out from its shelf Volume One of the *Topographic Anatomy* of Mssrs. Testut and Jacob (which, a thousand blessings upon it, has faithfully accompanied me for almost forty years)—the introduction to the section entitled "Neck." It reads:

The ancients believed that the neck increased its volume following the first sexual intercourse. . . . An epithalamium of Catullus says, speaking of a young bride:

> *Non illam nutrix, oriente luce revisens,*
> *Hesterno poterit collum circundare filo.*
> [Her nurse, upon seeing her at dawn the following day /
> No longer could surround her neck with the eve's riband.]

This tradition, according to Malgaigne, has survived to our day, for it is not difficult to find midwives who pretend to identify virginity by the simple expedient that follows: the circumference of the neck is taken at its midportion with a thread, and the length of this thread is doubled. The tips of the thread are held between the incisors, and the vertex of the head is spanned with the loop thus made. If the loop can be made to pass freely over the crown, it is a bad sign; if, by contrast, the loop is found too tight, this result favors virginity. We have no clear observations in this particular, and cannot vouch for the truth in the popular tradition. Malgaigne, without granting it great value, finds it not altogether unfounded. In effect, outside of cases of goiter or other pathologic neck deformity, this author assures us that he found the loop to be too tight in young girls aged between fifteen and twenty years whose customs allowed not the slightest suspicion. Petrequin, however, having repeated Malgaigne's experiment in several young girls, is not willing to accept his opinion.[16]

The power of words! I seriously doubt if I could remember all the muscles of the infrahyoid region, or the course and relations of the carotid artery and its branches, so painstakingly detailed by Testut and Jacob along 130 pages of dense, magnificently illustrated text. But the ancient belief in the expandability of the virginal female's neck, its portentous postcoital swelling, and the image of a Monsieur Malgaigne measuring the circumference of young maidens' white and delicate necks—these are the things I remember, after four decades, as clearly as if I had read them yesterday. And I fancy that I see Madame Bovary herself—Mademoiselle Rouault, more properly at the time—being asked by her straitlaced fiancé, who was, after all, a country physician, if she would be so kind as to submit to a painless measurement of cervical circumference "in the interest of science." Not, alas, that an overly loose loop would have discouraged him in his ill-fated designs. It is simply that a man naturally wishes to know, or at any rate, vehemently yearned to know, in those benighted days . . .

My hostess abruptly interrupts my daydreaming asking me whether I liked the exhibits. I mumble some stock phrases and thank her for her gracious courtesy with equally trite formulas. And all the while, much to my dismay, I realize I have been staring at her neck, so that by an automatic movement she covers it defensively with her right hand. I think she had a touch of goiter.

WAXING PHILOSOPHICAL...
AND A BIT HYPERSENSITIVE

Tissues preserved in chemical fixatives pose annoying problems. Strong fixatives, such as formalin, emit noxious fumes which themselves have the ability to fix cells ("and this includes the pathologist's," notes a technical manual); anyone who has shed tears in a room full of formalinized specimens would readily agree with all this. Moreover, the fixative solution must be renewed frequently. I recall no stronger reminder of the evolutionary superiority of yeasts and fungi over our proud species than the spectacle of mold growing freely inside jars containing specimens suspended in an alcohol-based fixative: the tough microorganisms had chosen the fixative for their nutrient broth! And then, there is the problem of specimen handling. No irritating chemical, regardless of its nature, must ever be touched with ungloved hands.

In view of these problems, it was inevitable that artificial models should have been thought of as appropriate substitutes for anatomical specimens preserved in fixatives. And among modeling materials, wax was a natural choice. In expert hands, wax may be used as medium to copy reality with astonishing faithfulness. The figures of old-fashioned wax museums have the power to move us with horror or delight; fully dressed, bejeweled, clad in tattered or sumptuous attire, and shown under carefully disposed lights, they seem to incarnate the "real" personages. We cannot distinguish the model from the true person, and we imagine that we face the latter, whom we find frozen, congealed in a state of suspended animation, asleep, or dead. Wax pushes the illusion of reality to an extreme and sometimes to an unbearable extreme.

Nowhere did the art of anatomical wax modeling receive as great an impetus, or reach as lofty heights, as in eighteenth-century Florence, particularly under the able hand of Abbot Felice Fontana (1730–1805), a cleric-naturalist who enjoyed the sponsorship of the Grand Duke of Tuscany. Under Fontana's guidance, artists and anatomists collaborated mutually with an intensity and fruitfulness seldom achieved.

Although the word *wax* today means various substances, including synthetic paraffins, in those days wax sculpture was done exclusively with the natural wax that bees secrete to make their cells in the hive. The Florentine wax shops themselves must have resembled a beehive in their bustling activity. A visitor would see workers in shirtsleeves and aprons occupied in removing the honey, melting the hives in hot water cauldrons, and eliminating the impurities by a laborious procedure that ended in obtaining virgin wax, a product whose color and consistency varied with the species and habitat of the bees. Other workers added animal fat or spermaceti (a solid waxy substance from sperm whales) to impart the right consistency to the material used in modeling. Still others, busily and somewhat ceremoniously, prepared the pigments: the trade had its own mystique, and the methods to color the wax were often the secret of the master ceroplast. Of course, there was much that was subjective, empirical, and vague in the procedures. Whitening was produced by exposure to sunlight or "by mixture with white lead and turpentine; yellow, with orpiment [a metal consisting mainly of arsenic trisulfide] and turpentine; golden, with red lead and turpentine; green, with verdigris; black, with crushed charcoal or cinnabar. . . ."[1]

In another room, anatomists and artists worked together. The former dissected a cadaver to adequately expose the chosen anatomical region. Liquid plaster was poured directly on the exposed structures, which were previously greased to avoid unwanted adherences. After hardening, the plaster was carefully detached, often in predetermined segments, a procedure facilitated by the prior placement of strings. Each concavity in the plaster faithfully corresponded to a protuberance of the specimen. This mold was greased, and molten wax was poured in: first a lightly colored layer, then, after solidification, a new layer, each time at a different temperature: this was made possible by altering the melting point of the wax through the addition of mixtures of pork fat, mutton fat, or resins. By this layering technique the most perfect reproduction of the transparency of living tissues was achieved.

With loving attention to detail, came the finishing touches. Every imperfection of the cast was carefully smoothed out; the surface of the modeled specimen was polished with turpentine-soaked brushes; the delicate striations of the muscles were simulated with tracings of a fine point. Tenuous, translucid membranous structures, like the omentum or the pericardium, were achieved by flattening the wax with a roller on a preheated marble slab. Tiny branches of lymphatics, delicate blood vessels, and minute radicles of nerves were rendered by means of threads soaked in wax; drops of wax made to slide along these lines would produce the small lymph nodes. Not the slightest concession to expediency was ever made if it meant detriment to the realism desired: eyebrows and eyelashes were authentic, implanted one by one on the appropriate site of the statue; and Lelli, the Bolognese artist, used real human skeletons as frames to support the muscles and soft tissues that he modeled.

The exquisite waxwork of the Florentine artists was first exhibited to the public in 1780, when La Specola Museum opened, then called Reale Museo di Fisica e Storia Naturale. In 137 showcases were exhibited 486 preparations along with 208 drawings in color, framed in ebony, many with explanatory legends in pretty calligraphy. Among the illustrious visitors to the museum was Joseph II, emperor of Austria, son (eldest

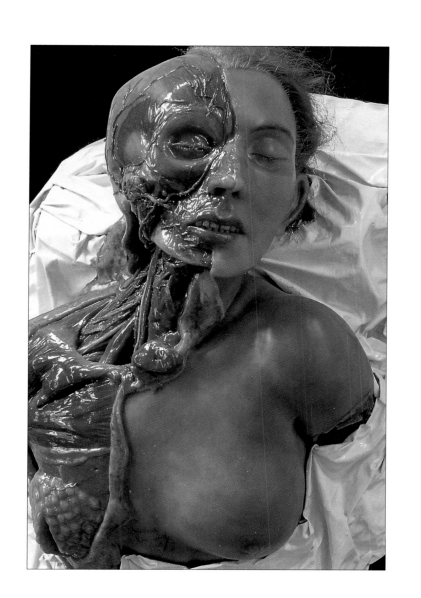

among five other sons and ten daughters) of Maria Theresa and Franz I, and brother to the famed and ill-fated Marie Antoinette, wife of France's Louis XVI. Cold, distrustful, sarcastic, and financially conservative to the point of niggardliness, Joseph II was also the epitome of the "enlightened despot."

The Austrian emperor visited Italy in the halcyon days of anatomical studies. In Bologna, he paid a personal homage to Anna Morandi. In Florence, his enthusiasm for the figures shown him by Fontana knew no bounds. He named Fontana Knight of the Holy Empire, and commissioned him with the execution of replicas of most of the wax models, especially those portraying obstetrical complications. Intending to promote medical teaching as no Austrian ruler had done before, he became convinced that obstetrics could be best learned through the study of wax models. The emperor had opened a school for military surgeons in Vienna, for which an imposing construction had been erected and placed under the direction of the physician-in-chief of the Imperial Army. This would be the seat of the collection.

A project of this magnitude was to Fontana's shop the equivalent of a modern corporation's landing a large-scale, highly remunerative contract. Rancor and envy followed immediately. The Grand Duke of Tuscany, led by the artist's enemies, took a dim view of the fact that his best artists and their resources were tied up in the service of a foreign sovereign. In the squabbles that followed, Fontana was forced to change domicile. But against discouraging odds, working indefatigably for about six years, 1,192 models were completed.

Complying with the emperor's request, many of these illustrated obstetrical and gynecological complications: some uteruses demonstrated a variety of pathological states, while others, with windows, showed the fetus in all the conceivable abnormal positions that may complicate birth. These models were crated, fastened on mules' backs, and, in 1786, sent off in two large convoys across the Brenner Pass and on to Linz, where the crates were transferred to barges that took them to Vienna.[2]

Every time I think of the voyage of Fontana's obstetrical models across the Alps and on the Danube River, I find it difficult to resist the facile, perhaps even trite association of ideas that link that journey with the notion of the "wandering womb." For it is an inalterable fact that men once believed sincerely that the uterus was a self-willed entity with a propensity to roam, to travel, which it could express within the confines of the female's body. Of all the preposterous notions that men have entertained over the years—and the number of these is infinite—none seems so incredible and bizarre. Blame for this irrational belief is laid at the door of Plato, who, in *Timaeus,* compared the sexual organs to frenzied animals prompt to disobey the orders of restraint emanating from "the seat of counsel," that is, the brain. He meant both male and female organs, and he was, of course, speaking metaphorically. But his language was powerful, his imagery vivid, and his vision inspired. Which is why his words were taken literally, and by the time the Hippocratic medical collection was consolidated, Greek medicine was ready to accommodate the womb's wanderlust.

Ancient Greek medicine viewed the body of woman as essentially porous, crisscrossed by a system of canals, or *phlebes,* through which the uterus could travel. Health, especially that pertaining to the sexual sphere, largely depended on permeability of the canals. Disease, in contrast, could originate from blockage or obstruction of these conduits. Imagine the *iatros,* the Greek physician, examining a female patient and trying to determine the cause of her sterility. His diagnostic investigation includes ascertainment of the patency of the *phlebes.* Therefore he investigates the patient's capacity to smell strong odoriferous compounds, in whose composition garlic figures prominently, through the mouth: clear passages would convey the smell to the nose. He now determines the patient's inability to pass the test and concludes that the basic cause of infertility is an obstruction of the canal system, therefore a blockage to the conveyance of the male seed. Asked for a diagnosis, I suppose he would say: "Her tubes are blocked."

There could be a confusing symptomatology. In that case, the physician would investigate the position of the uterus, that wanton, self-willed organ with an invincible proclivity for travel. Where could it go?

Preferentially to the heart, liver, and brain, organs of the greatest "moisture" and served by the widest *phlebes.* Having spotted the footloose womb away from its right and proper site, the physician had to implement the measures required to return it to its correct location. A therapeutic procedure consisted in applying foul-smelling substances to the woman's nostrils while she sat in a bowl filled with fragrant perfume. Presumably, the wayward uterus would be repelled by the evil scents and attracted to the pleasant ones, an expectation that implies belief not only in its inclination to roam, but also in its autonomous discernment and sentience, at least as regards the sense of smell.[3]

Fontana's "wandering wax wombs" reached their destination, Vienna. Here, the precious cargo was placed inside the building raised by Joseph II to house the school of military surgery, since known as Museum Josephinum. As many as eight hundred pieces survive, and many are exhibited in that city's museum of pathologic anatomy. Dusty, worn-out, tarnished by the passage of centuries, they have the look of things exhausted and no longer useful. In a sense they once lived, but their life cycle is now complete. Yet the hand that would destroy them, or the impulse to melt them down and be done with them, stops in midcourse with reverential respect. It is arrested by the realization that wax figures mark an important moment in scientific knowledge when men realized that in medicine the hand and the eye had constantly to verify every concept formerly developed in a purely abstract, deductive fashion.

Artists and medical scientists cooperated then, as they have not done since, to produce an image of the body that could pass for a perfect imitation of nature. This image, this imitation, turned out to have, in the words of Michel Lemire, "a troubling, sensual and surreal aspect, going well beyond the necessary scientific precision and the desired illusion."[2]

Ceroplasts and anatomists of the golden era of wax modeling handed us no less than "an eternally transmissible model of the human body" (Lemire). Indeed, every age has fashioned its own model. The Greeks a porous one, riddled with *phlebes* through which the uterus could travel; the Middle Ages an even airier one, for the bodily conduits were filled with ethereal "humors," like disembodied spirits, and the uterus appeared subdivided into seven compartments—precisely seven, a mystical number, as the cabalists insisted; and the Enlightenment a starkly realistic, three-dimensional one, in which the transparence, the opalescence, and even the tactile quality of the skin or the humidity of exposed flesh were successfully imitated by the expert use of wax.

And our age? What is the model of the human body that we have made? Paradoxically, an even subtler one, airier and more abstract than any dreamed by medieval *medici*. It is the image of colored blotches that the body traces by its temperature, as shown in thermography; of vector forces that are revealed in films through magnetic resonance; of atomic energy disclosed in positron-emission imaging. For the more refined our methods, the more the true nature of the body escapes us; the more it seems to constantly recede before us, to melt away—like wax?—and elude our understanding. So that the progressively subtler models that we construct appear ultimately to lead to what Paul Valéry called the "fourth body": a body that is as one with the environment, just as a vortex existing in the water held by a glass is distinct from the water, yet indistinguishable from it. Medieval philosophers would have loved our model. They contended that the material human body is accidental, its real nature residing in impalpable "essences" that transcend corporeality. We are not far removed from this idea, since we seem to have concluded that we are, as I think Bertrand Russell once put it, mere "collections of electromagnetic phenomena."

Ceroplasty, however, was only an imitation of nature. The other method created to preserve anatomical structure was more ambitious, since it aimed to perpetuate the concrete existence of real organs and tissues. This was achieved by intravascular injection of fixatives and dyes. By delivering these compounds into blood vessels, and thus into the most recondite parts of the anatomy, admirable preparations were obtained. The technique reached its apogee in the eighteenth century, with Frederik Ruysch (1638–1731), professor of anatomy at the Atheneum Illustre of Amsterdam. Like many of his colleagues at the time, Ruysch seemed driven not by purely scientific interest, but also by a strange and morbid temperament.

Vascular injection was probably the most fruitful technique in biomedical research at the start of the eighteenth century.[4] Researchers fiercely vied with each other to exploit its potential and devise improvements, just as their modern counterparts today would stake their good names, and would sell their souls to the devil, to be first in laying their hands on the latest ultramicroscope or newest positron-emission equipment. But the most widespread attitude toward the aims of research was very different in the baroque age. Consider Frederik Ruysch and his personal collection.[5] Five rooms of his house at the Niewe Zijds Achterburgwal in Amsterdam were filled with the specimens he had prepared. It was a true museum, open to friends, students, and important visitors. In the first room there were twenty-five skeletons of infants and children. Only these were not simply classified and arranged in a monotonous numbered series, as might be expected for didactic displays of the era. Quite the contrary: they were disposed in lively tableaux. One skeleton seemed to be playing a violin made of dried tissues, while another struck a dolorous pose, as if weeping, holding against its face a large handkerchief made of peritoneal membrane. Baroque adornments decorated Ruysch's skeletons and mummified corpses: mayflies, strings of pearls, small candles, and star-shaped melon seeds attached to bones, looped around vertebrae, or hung from phalanxes. Skulls flaunted their empty orbits or stared at the visitor with shiny glass eyeglobes patiently prepared by the curator. And these eerie, disquieting little personages, frozen in the middle of some fantastic stageplay, sent an all too obvious moralizing message. A child's skeleton, its skull filled with cotton, pointed its discarnate finger at a sign that read: *Vita humana lusus* (Human life is but a game). Another one sat amidst a fantastic landscape in which leafless trees were inverted, ramifying dried aortas or tracheobronchial tubes; rocks were figured by gallstones and distended viscera; and in this surrealistic scene a skeleton held a sign that said: *Vita quid est? Fumus fugiens et bulla caduca* (What is life? Transient smoke and perishable bubble).

In another room of Ruysch's "Cabinet," there were fifty preparations in liquid fixative, and a few dried. Like most anatomists who performed intravascular injections, Ruysch kept the formulas of his fluids zealously guarded. Historians of medicine have given full accounts of the technical details of his ministrations. A French spiritous beverage, brandy of Nantes, or "Nantic Brandy," as it was referred to, was an important component of his fixative, or, in Ruysch's fancy term, his *liquor balsamicus*. After injecting various mixtures and dyes, depending on the result desired, striking preparations could be obtained. Thus, membranous structures in which lymphatic and vascular networks were revealed could be made to look like pieces of fine, delicate lacework. Ruysch's goal was to give to his cadavers and specimens a perfect appearance of life: the color, the tone, the freshness of youth. And his achievement in this singular deception, which might have made modern embalmers pale with envy, he wished to put at the service of his moralizing ideals.

He was not content with embalming the corpse of a fetus: he thought it necessary to dress it with a laced gown, which his wife and diligent assistant, Maria Post, or his daughter, Rachel, would obligingly sew. The embalmed arm of a child was covered by a quaint little batiste sleeve before being placed in a jar. The jar itself was sealed with lacquer and lead foil, and then topped with a stretched pig's bladder. Adding to the striking effect of his preparations was his preference for placing fixed specimens in attitudes that simulated some activity: a hand was made to hold an eye by the optic nerve, between index finger and thumb; an arm encircled a uterus, as if carrying it; the skull of a prostitute, bearing pathologic marks of syphilis, was put in the same jar with a baby's leg, which seemed to be kicking it contemptuously. All these odd and often gruesome compositions were immensely popular with his contemporaries, who were inured to art forms centered upon the idea of the transitoriness of human life, the "Vanities," and utterly familiar with the varied symbolism thereof. So it was that Ruysch's collection was vaunted as "a perfect necropolis, all the inhabitants of which were asleep and ready to speak as soon as they were awakened." The great Fontenelle wrote an essay in praise of the Dutch anatomist, the *Eloge de Ruysch,* which another panegyrist paraphrased, rhapsodizing with lyrical accents: "His mummies were a revelation of life, compared with which those of the Egyptians presented but the vision of death. Man seemed to continue to live in the one, and to continue to die in the other." Giacomo Leopardi (1798–1837), an Italian poet with a morbid obsession with death, wrote a short piece or *Operetta Morale,* in which he imagined Ruysch having a philosophical conversation with his mummies on the essence of death.[6]

One morning, amidst great commotion and fanfare, who appeared at Ruysch's Cabinet, but Peter the Great, Czar of all Russias! He signed the *Album Amicorum* in the first room and roamed through the strange collection. He was utterly delighted. The fetal skeleton that pointed at a pregnant uterus preserved intact with its developing four-month-old fetus, while saying: "No nobler grave could have held it"; the mummified corpses with beads, flower wreaths, and lace garments floating in *liquor balsamicus;* and the collection of fixed female genital organs with the appearance of undisturbed naturalness, which our Calvinist-burgher and injector-anatomist kept in his *Thesauri Anatomici*—displays such as these, sent the Czar into ecstasy. It is said that he kissed the cheek of an embalmed cadaver of a child that seemed to be in deep sleep. So great was the impression left in the mind of the Russian potentate, that he insisted on coming back in 1717, on the occasion of another visit to the Netherlands. He greeted Ruysch with the words: "You are still my old mentor," and proceeded to offer to buy the entire collection, including the formulas for the liquid fixatives and the protocols of the various methods used in the preparations, for the then unbelievable price of thirty thousand Dutch guldens. The deal was signed promptly.

Of the approximately two thousand items cataloged, only half reached their Russian destination due to the perils and hazards of travel in those days. The story is told that many specimens deteriorated because the preserving fluid was not renewed opportunely, on account of the sailors having drunk the Nantic Brandy essential for the preparation of *liquor balsamicus.* This version is promptly dismissed as spurious by a modern commentator on the reasonable assumption that the Czar's well-known temper would have deterred such irregular practices. Be that as it may, after two world wars, nine hundred specimens were mentioned in an inventory drawn in 1947 in the Kirov Academy of Leningrad. Many are still on exhibit at the Kunstkammer of this city, where visitors may be amazed by the power to simulate life that the ancient techniques of vascular injection still demonstrate more than 260 years after their first application.

Despite all these achievements, the technique of intravascular injection, like ceroplasty and the public performance of dissection, ceased to be a topic of general interest. It is not idle to ask why this happened. On the surface, the answers seem obvious: better methods of teaching anatomy were devised, the importance of macroscopic anatomy diminished, other concerns occupied the minds of researchers, and the like. But nothing of what is human is ever fully explainable by simple answers, and the reasons why these developments took place may reside in much more complex social and psychological interactions.

It is very true that ceroplasty and intravascular injection were devised in response to practical needs, such as the urgency to preserve the decaying organs and tissues of a corruptible cadaver. But at the same time, these techniques reflected a newly acquired sensitivity, a new mentality that found the spectacle of death and corruptibility offensive, repugnant, and unbearable. It is no coincidence that these developments took place at the same time as the Romantic movement was crystallizing in literature and the plastic arts. Romanticism extolled delicacy of sentiment over the earthy materiality of past eras. Giovanna Ferrari quotes paragraphs of Jean-Jacques Rousseau and moving pages of Goethe, in which these two towering figures of the Romantic movement give free vent to their horror of anatomical dissection, an activity that they found "barbaric" and profoundly contemptible.[7]

Although Goethe's name is appropriately invoked to buttress claims that artists contributed to the shaping of the new collective sensibility, it is often overlooked that the German poet was an outright advocate of ceroplasty, and a very vocal one. It must be recalled he was deeply interested in the natural sciences, to the point of having written a treatise on the theory of colors. His advocacy of anatomical modeling was entered in *Wilhelm Meisters Wanderjahre,* "The Travels of William Meister," the novel that occupied him in the last decade of his life: it was published in his seventy-second year, fifty years after *The Sorrows of Young Werther*. The word *Wanderjahre* refers to the period of traveling that German artisans were obligated to undertake, either by law or by tradition, after their formal apprenticeship (*Lehrjahre*) had been completed.

In an episode of the novel, the protagonist, a young man who pursues anatomical studies as part of his quest for ideal perfection, is given an arm to dissect. It happens to be the delicate, white, gracile arm of a recently drowned maiden. In a duly romantic passage, the would-be dissector contemplates the beautiful upper limb, muses over the melancholy fact that, only days before, that arm might have enfolded the neck of the girl's young lover, and lets the scalpel fall from his hand, lacking the strength to carry out his assigned task. The entire scene is watched by a mysterious man, also attending the anatomy course. He bids the shaken dissector to follow him, and, once in his shop, reveals himself as an artist, a *plastischer Anatom* who devotes his most earnest efforts to the construction of anatomical models. Goethe, through the mouth of his fictional personage, can now exalt the noble aims of a branch of human industry that tries to imitate life and to create lifelike structures, instead of teasing, cutting, rending, or dissecting corpses, which is like adding an extra measure of death to what is dead already.

Goethe's enthusiasm for anatomical wax sculpture, so lively that he was prompted to write a letter to a member of Parliament recommending the promotion of this art in Germany,[8] must have stemmed from his direct encounter with the productions of the great wax modelers during his Italian journeys. But his pleas to abandon anatomical dissection in favor of the study of models were not based exclusively on pragmatic or technical considerations. Like other romantic artists, he appealed to superior ideals of beauty, to supra-individual norms that must govern the actions of all human beings who aspire to perfection. The "new man" was a sensitive, delicate being, unable to countenance the spectacle of bloodshed and organic decomposition. Models in wax, being highly realistic imitations, superb artificial contrivances, managed to cleave a deep chasm between death's horrid aspects and the student. Most commendably, they were supposed to do this without detriment to the quest for knowledge.

Coping with the spectacle of a decomposing cadaver has been difficult in all ages. However, past generations were able to establish a certain communion with the dead, a certain intimate commerce that seems no longer possible. Callous insensitivity, unfortunately, was one manifestation of the former attitude. Recall that crowds watched with relish public executions, torture, and dismemberment. At the dawn of the seventeenth century, the same crowds that cheered the quartering of the regicide Ravaillac—torn limb by limb in a Paris plaza by teams of horses pulling in separate directions while an executioner poured molten lead down his throat—also filled the amphitheaters where anatomical dissection was performed.

Death was not, as in our days, a spectral, terrifying image whose presence must not be evoked in polite conversation. It was a harrowing, but concrete, everyday reality. Consequently, the realm of the dead and the ambiance of the living were not cleft from each other as they are now, but closely adjoined each other. A lithograph by Goya shows a woman endeavoring to pull out the teeth of a man who has recently been hanged and is still suspended by the rope. Presumably, she did this because the teeth of a hanged man were used as amulets against evil or as ingredients in medicinal preparations. In England and elsewhere, teeth, skin, fat, hair, or other parts of the body of executed criminals were valued as remedies for various ailments, and entered in the composition of potions and preparations of folk medicine. Assuredly, all this was base superstition. But it shows how intimately the world of the living and the world of the dead interpenetrated each other. The presence of the departed prolonged itself in time not as mere residual image in the memory, but as a concrete, tangible object for the living to perceive.

Wax modeling was the first successful effort we undertook to distance ourselves from the dead. Since then, we have not ceased in our efforts to deepen the gulf.

HOW WE COME TO BE

THE WAY WE USED TO . . .

Man and woman contribute to conception, but what surprises in the male's participation is its fleetingness. It seems flashing and paroxysmal. Episodically driven by the violence of his powerful sexual desire, which is the desire of desires, the male deposits his seed—a viscid, whitish secretion, which is the secretion of secretions. Aristotle saw in it the quintessential humor, a refined product made not of crass and earthy matter, like most objects in the world, but of water and *pneuma*. The Greeks thus believed it to be a foam, an ethereal vehicle for the creative force of nature.

In his work, *Generation of Animals,* Aristotle vindicates the transitory nature of the male contribution and ascribes to semen the most extraordinary qualities.[1] Woman provides the material, man the energy that molds it into form. The raw material furnished by the mother is blood, a surfeit of which exists, anyway, since it must flow out monthly. Semen, on the other hand, supplies a principle of movement, *kinesis,* which ought not to be confused with purely physical motion, for it is rather an organizing principle, like the architectural plan by which a house is built, semen is "movement in actuality" (734b, 7–17). Just as the genius of the sculptor is communicated to the rough block of marble that becomes the statue of Hermes, so is "form" transmitted via the father's semen to the conceptus. And just as nothing in the sculptor's tools passes on to his production, so "semen is not a part of the fetus as it develops" (730b 11). Likewise, a life-giving "heat" exists in semen, but it should not be understood as mere ordinary heat: it is instead the kind of life-giving energy that resides in the sun, which upon hitting a piece of rotting organic matter brings forth all manner of living creatures—who has not seen worms emerge from a damp, rotting tree trunk in the woods when the sun's rays contact it? And since the sun is a star, it is no hyperbole to claim that semen embodies a quintessence analogous to that of the stars!

That semen emerges from base excretory organs must have irked the Greek sensibility. Surely, the semidivine properties of this fluid demanded a daintier outlet. And since the Greek regard for ratiocination placed the brain uppermost in the hierarchy of the organs, a reconciling physiology was not long in coming: semen originates in the brain. Pythagoras taught that semen is "a drop of brain containing hot vapor within it." These two components were, in the Pythagorean scheme, physiologically distinct.

When brought to the womb "flesh, sinews, bones, hair, and the whole of the body [of the fetus]" form from its gel-like portion, "while soul and sense come from the vapor within it."[2]

Aristotle takes up again this ponderous question in his *Problemata*. Problem IV: Why do the eyes and the hips hollow out visibly in those who indulge to excess in venereal pleasure, even though the eyes are far and the hips close to the genital organs? Answer: Because the region of the eyes is, of all the parts of the head, that which forms most sperm. During coition, remarks our metaphysician-turned-physiologist, it is the eyes that alter most noticeably, and it is the eyes that appear sunken in those who abuse sexual intercourse. "The cause being that the nature of semen is similar to that of the brain, for its matter is aqueous and its warmth is acquired."[3]

In the Middle Ages, we see Albertus Magnus, the teacher of Thomas Aquinas, retaking the Aristotelian "problem" and adding picturesque observations of his own. To the question *Utrum magis derivetur sperma ab una parte quam alia* (whether sperm comes mainly from one [bodily] part than another), the answer, as expected, is "especially from the brain, whose substance corresponds to that of semen by its whiteness, softness, and humidity." To my eye, the "proof" adduced by Albertus Magnus is less abstract than the lucubrations of the Stagirite and vastly surpasses them in color: immersion of the testes of an inebriated man in cold water (ice-cold, I like to imagine) promptly restores him to sobriety.

Nor is Albert short of precedents. Clement of Bohemia reported that a monk had died in a state of emaciation, as a consequence of having "desired" sixty-two times a lady of quality before matins. Because the monk belonged to an aristocratic family, an autopsy was done; for autopsies, historians assure us, were sometimes practiced for medico-legal reasons during the Middle Ages.[4] The brain was found profoundly atrophied, reduced to the size of a pomegranate. The eyes were destroyed. *Ergo,* Albertus Magnus was right: coition empties preferentially the brain.

Dear to the Middle Ages was the physiological theory of the four humors: yellow bile, black bile, blood, and phlegm. Semen was not one of the four; it was a derivative, a product of purification and refinement. If not a distillate of brain substance, at least an extract of the blood, the sap of the tree of life. Of the high and mighty qualities of semen there was never any doubt, a fact that has not escaped the fulminations of contemporary feminists, particularly when contrasted with the historically low position of the maternal contribution to conception. Toward the end of the thirteenth century, Giles of Rome, the *Doctor Fundatissimus* of the Augustinians, emphasized the warmth of semen, that *thermos athmos* or vaporous warmth of which Pythagoras spoke. Semen was "blood twice cooked," but in a state that fell short of the last degree of concoction, otherwise it would be impeded from reaching the testicles. Warmth, in its association with semen, betokened a fundamental quality of maleness. Dispossessed of this quality, women could never bring the germ to its optimal degree of "coction." Women were deemed to embody a quality of coldness, and for this very reason they could produce, by themselves, only imperfect conceptions. The idea of the quintessential nature of semen is perhaps as old as the history of civilization. Aulus Celsus, Roman encyclopedist under Tiberius, compendiously declared that "the ejaculation of semen is the casting away of part of the soul"— *Seminis emissio est partes anima jactura.*

Together with Aristotelian ideas, a different and sometimes contrary system of biomedical concepts arose in antiquity; it was to endure for centuries. This was the Galenic system, for which quantitative and qualitative abnormalities of semen were defined forms of pathology. Galen's reference to the shocking conduct of the Cynic philosopher Diogenes is of some interest in this context, since it portrays a more sanguine attitude toward ejaculation. According to Galen, Diogenes "passed for having been the firmest of men in any endeavor that demanded fixity of purpose and continence; but he indulged venereal pleasure, wishing to unburden himself of the discomfort that produces a retained sperm, not seeking after the pleasure that accompanies its emission." According to Galen, Diogenes asked a courtesan to meet him one day, and upon her being late "he freed his own seed with his hand." The courtesan then arrived, but the philosopher sent her away, telling her: "My hand arrived at the hymeneal celebration earlier than you."[5]

This relatively casual observation of Galen on the potential benefit of self-induced ejaculation of a surfeit of semen was to be opposed with extraordinary rigor and fierce indignation by the early Christian theologians. Curious to remark, their horror of masturbation has been matched in intensity only by the medical profession's abhorrence of the solitary vice in relatively recent times. Christian condemnation was based on biblical interpretation. An express prohibition is spelled out in Holy Writ against the crime of Onan, who let his seed fall on the ground, and was slain by the Lord in punishment for his misconduct (*Genesis* 38: 6–10). Later, the idea of its evil was further compounded. Masturbation became not only a sin against nature, *vitium contra naturam,* but its repugnant quality was magnified by the panoply of sinful mental representations that are its regular concomitants. Hence, theologians commented that those who masturbate often do so while simultaneously "desiring" the carnal union with a partner whose very existential condition adds a new dimension to the first sin; for if a married woman is desired, to the initial turpitude is added adultery; if a virgin, rape; if a relative, incest; and if a nun, sacrilege. In the nineteenth century, a Monsignor Bouvier, high prelate of the Church, added one more convolution to this list of depravities: if the Virgin Mary is the object of imaginary concupiscence, the extra sin becomes "horrendous sacrilege," *horrendum sacrilegium.*[6] I take it that only the ascetic mind is fit to devise true refinement to unsophisticated intemperance; it is perhaps no coincidence that a monsignor should have come up with a turn worthy of the Marquis de Sade in his dungeon.

In the Galenic doctrine, semen is not only a male secretion stored in the testes. There is also a female generative fluid, and it is stored in the *testes muliebres,* or "testes of women," as Vesalius called the ovaries. These glands, located deep in the female pelvis, are the counterpart of the male gonads. It did not escape the sagacity of the ancients that a whole system of anatomical and functional equivalences between the sexes may be educed from the genital system. Thus, Galen believed that a fluid female seed traveled in the fallopian tubes to reach the ovaries, just as semen found its testicular storage site after traveling in the epididymides, male ducts which, in fact, are embryologically the counterparts of the fallopian tubes. Today, we do not believe in the existence of a "female semen," but perhaps we should: a diffusible chemical factor, probably a small peptide, is suspected of being secreted by the ovaries to "beckon" sperm.[7]

Galenic medicine went further in its systematization of the generative function. It attributed considerable importance to the right-left opposition of paired gonads. The right spermatic vein, like the right ovarian vein, drains directly into the inferior vena cava, which in turn courses through the liver. The left-sided vessels, in contrast, drain into the renal venous system. The liver, which was believed to possess a metaphysical "warmth," is on the right side. Warmth was a male quality. Therefore a privileged position was acknowledged to right-sided organs: the right-sided gonads were likelier to generate males; left-sided organs, being colder, received humors apt to determine the female sex of the offspring.[8]

Nor can it be said that the opposition between Galenic and Aristotelian thought was purely academic. A perceptive contemporary historian, Jean-Louis Flandrin, has defined the practical consequences of adhering to one or the other theories of conception.[9] Because Christian doctrine maintains that the goal of sexual union is not pleasure, but procreation, it became very important to decide on the place of sensual pleasure in the generative act. But sexual pleasure is a physiological phenomenon. What did the medical authorities have to say? In the Galenic system, women emit a "fluid seed," just like men; and this emission was seen as pleasurable to women, just as ejaculation is indissolubly linked to pleasure in men. For conception to occur, said Galen, there must be an admixture of male and female seeds. It follows that in the Galenic system an embryo was always the result of shared pleasure. Therefore, Christian moralists ought to condemn sexual intercourse if the woman feels no pleasure.

The practical consequences were altogether different in the Aristotelian view of generation. For the Stagirite, the female contribution to conception is only menstrual blood, upon which the male seed exerts its portentous organizing powers. Therefore women play a purely passive role, furnishing a fluid that is shed regularly and whose emission is not in itself pleasurable. Therefore feminine pleasure is not indispensable to procreation.

An entire edifice of sexual or matrimonial morality could be constructed following one or the other thinker's ideas. Is it morally permissible to resort to techniques that prolong the sexual act? Yes, if the goal is to provoke the simultaneous discharge of male and female seeds, thereby promoting procreation. No, if it is believed that feminine pleasure is independent of the ability to conceive. It is a fact of common observation that many women conceive without experiencing pleasure. On the other hand, the all-too-visible reality of feminine pleasure could not be denied and required a rational interpretation. Why should God have decreed a pleasurable feminine sexual experience? As Flandrin puts it, too much Aristotelianism might have undermined the very foundations of Christian teachings on human sexuality.[10] Although a thoroughgoing Aristotelianism is triumphant in Saint Jerome, Saint Augustine, and other great doctors of the Church, the Galenic viewpoint prevailed in European medical writings of the sixteenth and seventeenth centuries. At length, theologians borrowed from one or the other system according to their individual needs and in the manner deemed most helpful to the advancement of their own preconceptions. Feminine sexual pleasure came to be regarded by many authorities as not indispensable for conception, but useful to upgrade the quality of the conceptus. It was believed that the offspring conceived amidst shared passionate effusions was healthier, stronger, and more perfect.

Upon the advent of modernity, semen lost much of its former prestige. The importance of the egg became abundantly demonstrated, first in avian, then in mammalian experiments. Men of science became "ovists," that is, upholders of the theory that all the parts of an embryo exist somehow preformed in the egg, waiting only for the stimulus of the male seed to expand and manifest themselves. No individual is formed *de novo*, that is to say, "from scratch." To all appearances, living beings are formed *ex ovo*, for God in his infinite wisdom had compressed and encapsulated the germs of all living things within the first female of each species. It remained to be shown, however, by what mechanism these compressed, abbreviated, and encapsulated rudiments could be made to expand.

Foremost champion of ovism was the Dutch physician Reinier de Graaf (1641–1673). The "feminine testicles," he affirmed, are the ovaries; and these contain eggs, just like the ovaries of birds. In effect, unassisted by the microscope, de Graaf identified as "eggs" the masses of cells that surround the oocyte, or egg cell, which is fertilized by the sperm during conception. Medicine acknowledges his insightful researches by attaching his name to the fluid-filled ovarian vesicles or follicles in which these cells are contained, the "Graafian follicles." De Graaf went further in his comparison between bird's eggs and human ovaries. Albumin, as is well-known, exists in the white of the eggs. And so it is that, when de Graaf subjected the liquor present in the follicles to the action of fire, "it acquired, by concoction, the same color, the same flavor, the same consistence as the white of hen's eggs." Voltaire's lampoon is at the ready: in one of his "Philosophical Dialogues" he says through the mouth of Evhemère: "a woman is but a white hen in Europe and a black hen in the heart of Africa."[11]

In the midst of this scientific climate, a certain Mr. Louis Ham came to visit the Dutch draper and haberdasher-turned-microscopist Antonie van Leeuwenhoek. The visitor carried a tube containing semen—not his own, he was quick to add with a Dutch burgher's *pruderie,* but from an involuntary, nocturnal ejaculation of a man afflicted with gonorrhea. Leeuwenhoek peeked through his rudimentary microscope, and the rest is history, as the popular saying goes. "Animalcules," "spermatick worms," "fish," "frogs," "tadpoles," or as we now call them, spermatozoa, tiny eel-like living creatures with long tails darted across the drop of semen, swimming briskly in all directions, and reminding a scholar of the times of nothing so much as "frogs before their limbs are formed."

We are not conceived *ex ovo,* the naturalists could now affirm, but *ex animalculo.* Wonder of wonders, the preformed germ exists in strange animalcules that are not part of the female seed, but of the male's. And whereas the preformed germ cannot manifest itself without ova, it is nonetheless true that it is an attribute of the male of the species. If one reflects ever so little on this matter, one must conclude, as did a savant of those times, that the ejaculation of semen is a "male parturition," since a preformed conceptus is thereby expelled. Bishop Garden, learned man that he probably was, insisted that biologic theory illuminated with splendiferous meaning the Messianic prophecy "that only Jesus is the true seed of Woman, and all the rest of mankind is the seed of man."[12]

Spectacular as it undoubtedly was, the "animalculist" theory of generation was short-lived. After a period of wild enthusiasm when observers believed they could distinguish in animalcules two sexes, varied configurations, and even habits and customs (the animalcules of sheep, for instance, were said to advance in closely massed "flocks" toward the womb), the spermatic little animals fell into discredit. For one thing, to accept the proposition that our exalted human species originates from tadpole-like creatures was distinctly unflattering. Then, the theory required of its adherents that they accept a number of inferences that did violence to common sense. If a tiny, complete embryo or homunculus is all wadded up inside each sperm cell, as shown in the famous illustration by Nicholas Hartsoeker (published in 1711), then one must assume that this tiny embryo, in turn, harbors its own embryo-containing sperm cells; and these, in turn, possess their own, and so on. Members of humankind would be boxed-in, like Russian dolls, one generation inside the other. But when one considers the enormous difference in size between a man and a sperm cell, it is evident that the size of the homunculus in only two or three generations must needs be smaller than the tiniest atom. What about in the many generations since Adam? The demands placed by this theory upon animalculists' credulity were simply too much!

Of course, much the same objections could be raised against the belief that a preformed embryo was contained in the egg. According to the "ovist" preformation theory, Eve had carried in her ovaries all the individuals born and to be born: the totality of humankind. One of the upholders of this theory, the Dutch scientist and mentor of de Graaf, Jan Swammerdam (1637–1680), believed that the boxed-in generations were limited in number: the end of humankind would come about upon the birth of the last of the preformed germs, that is, last of the boxed-in generations. Swammerdam knew, as the American vernacular puts it, that you have to draw the line somewhere.

It must be noted, however, that preformationism had distinct theological implications. Abbot Jean Senebier in the prologue to the experimental work of Spallanzani wrote: "There is not a man, not a plant, not an animalcule in a puddle which has not existed, and I might almost say lived for six thousand years [the length of time since Creation, according to some theologians' interpretation of Scripture], and which since then has not experienced a successive development in the bosom of the females. . . . Sacred history teaches us that God stopped creating at the end of the sixth day. Daily experience teaches us that God creates nothing new."[13]

Whether one belonged to the ovist or the animalculist persuasion, and whether one believed in a preformed germ or in an embryo that shapes up gradually from an amorphous rudiment (epigenesis), one could do no less than stand in awe of the wondrous powers of semen. And just as the grains, the seeds, and the pollens of flowering plants are shed into the air and conveyed by wind currents across considerable distances, could not the seeds of man also fill the air and be swept away and scattered by the wind to accomplish their unique brand of pollination, that is, fertilization? Heracleitus had taught long before that a divine soul or life-giving principle suffused the atmosphere and was sucked into our bodies with our every breath. Virgil poetically expressed this idea when he spoke, in his *Georgics,* about Andalusian mares that could be impregnated by the wind: "in spring, when their vital heat returns, they raise their heads, stand facing the West atop the cliffs, and snuff the light zephyr, and often without need to copulate are made pregnant, marvelous to recount. . . . (Book III, verses 272–275).

Medieval theologians maintained that in the state of innocence before the fall, man and woman could generate progeny by a simple effort of the will, entirely without physical contact; but after the fall they were forced to resort to the vile congress of their "shameful parts" in order to perpetuate the species. A little of such pristine generative powers inhered in sperm, in the *aura seminalis.* At least this was implied by those who insisted that the germ seeds floated in the air, invisible, after they had dried out, and could move about, wafted by the winds, carried here, there, and everywhere. They were as ubiquitous as the motes that one sees suspended and eddying about in midair when one lets a sun ray fall across a darkened room. The seeds for insemination had universal dissemination: this could have been a motto for subscribers to the theory of "panspermia," that most peculiar obsession.

But if the air is replete with floating germs or embryo-forming particles, and we, so to speak, immersed to our crowns in a sea of invisible animalcules, do these seeds ever germinate? They do, just like the seeds of plants, when they chance to land on the proper terrain. Even late in the eighteenth century, learned men asserted that certain women could be made pregnant by merely smelling the floating sperm: *Aliquot virgines tantum ad seminis odorem concipiunt.* In modified form, these strange beliefs survive to our day. A former colleague of mine in Kingston, Ontario, now retired, used to tell us that, in his youth, a stern head nurse severely forbade young nurses to swim in the same swimming pool where male hospital interns had cavorted hours before. She was utterly persuaded that floating germs could remain in the water without loss of their inseminating power and might cause accidental pregnancies in the unsuspecting young maidens.

In 1771, the expert testimony of faculty members of the ancient school of medicine of Montpellier served to exculpate a married woman charged with adultery after having conceived several years after separation from her legal husband. This case had originally been reviewed by jurisconsults of the Parliament of Grenoble, who concluded that the cause of the pregnancy had been the lady's powerful imagination: she reported having experienced a vivid dream, during which she saw her husband and mentally represented his embrace. The doctors of Montpellier, having discarded as superstitious the belief in the power of the imagination to cause pregnancy, went on to provide a scientific basis to the facts of the case, according to the latest concepts of reproductive biology. Exoneration of the woman was appropriate, but had to be buttressed on updated scientific knowledge. She had slept near the window. In the course of her sleep she became agitated under the influence of her dream. Tossing about in bed, she set the sheets in disarray: her body was exposed; the zephyr blew through the window and attained bodily parts that ordinarily would have been shielded by the bedcovers. And by this fortuitous circumstance, "organic molecules," "spermatick germs," "floating embryos," or "human insects" had insinuated themselves into the parts of her anatomy that are the substratum of the generative function. One of these eventually became the healthy newborn infant that the lady innocently begot.[14]

So much subtlety of reasoning satisfied but few. Some were sincerely amazed that human ingenuity succeeded in unveiling mysteries thereto unseen and worlds beyond the reach of our unaided senses. Skeptics, however, gloated in uncharitable puns and sarcastic allusions. It was one

thing to see the zephyr sung by Virgil blowing upon chaste wives, who thereafter became mothers in the style of the Latin poet's bucolic mares, and quite another thing to recollect the favorite method by which many women refresh themselves who later become pregnant in the absence of their husbands. But the truth is, in the state of scientific advancement of those times the mechanism of conception was too subtle for human understanding. This formidable problem surpassed the capacity of the best minds. Centuries after the discovery of spermatozoa, and long after it was established that both sperm and ova are indispensable to procreation, the phenomena of fertilization and embryonic growth and development remained submerged in the most complete obscurity. The keenest philosophers, the most penetrating intellects, Voltaire among them, resignedly confessed that there were things best left to the unfathomable workings of Providence. All that sensible men and women could do was to continue making babies as they had done from time immemorial: lustily, in unthinking abandon, and forsaking all hope of ever modifying or controlling the generative function.

This blessed ignorance would not last. It is not in mankind's proclivities to let things go unexamined, much less when human suffering is at stake. For in human procreation a generally pleasurable tumbling culminates in the drama of birth. "Drama" is a trite but uniquely appropriate word, since despite its stereotyped repetition down the ages, for millions of years, the birth of a human being carries in it something of the exorbitant, the disproportionate, and the unsettling. Life's eclosion may be saluted with lyrical stanzas, and the advent of new life celebrated with moving hymns; still, the flaming jewel has a shady side. Birth is a wrenching, a dislocation, an abrupt dehiscence: mother and child, until then intimately joined, are thereby divided. The scission is inevitable, inexorable, and irreversible—the very properties of death. Like death, birth is also an equalizer. As birth begins, the fetus descends from its undistinguished enclave between the bladder and the rectum. At birth we must pass between the reservoirs of urine and feces, since nature placed the maternal womb behind the bladder and in front of the rectum: *inter faeces et urinam nascimur.* All men, however exalted, start their lives thus. Bossuet could rightly declaim in one of his homilies: "Of whatever superb distinctions men are flattered, they all have the same origin, and this origin is little."[15]

The fetal descent is felt by the mother as an intolerable burden, an unbearable encumbrance or obstruction that must be cleared at all costs. Her forehead is sprinkled with a fine dew; her muscles tense; her mouth is dry; and she tosses about in perpetual restlessness: she is "in labor." Her friends or relatives comfort her and must sometimes restrain her jactitation. Nevertheless she moans, and perhaps she screams. She screams sometimes from pain, and sometimes obeying the cultural determinants of the expression of pain. No matter: from the humblest peasant to the haughtiest empress, the steps are the same, without exception. Like death, birth is the Great Leveler. Marie de Médicis, Queen of France, made great efforts to master her desire to scream during her labor. The midwife advised her to scream, "for fear that her throat might swell." And the king, realizing that his exalted spouse strove mightily to keep a trace of royal dignity in the midst of a harsh travail witnessed by a roomful of courtiers as demanded by custom, piteously bent over his suffering wife to tell her: "Scream, my friend, scream as the midwife tells you, so that your throat shall not swell. . . ."[16]

It is a struggle, a hand-to-hand combat. The fetus must relinquish the womb in the end, and cease to be a fetus to become an infant, but it was not always seen as a passive object: for a long time the fetus was supposed to be an active participant in the feto-maternal disjunctive struggle. At the end of nine months, went the old reasoning, the fetus is tired of its enclaustration. And it is hungry: it must go out to procure itself a substantive nourishment, a good, solid bite, for a change. Or else its habitation has become uncomfortable: dirty with its own accumulated urine and feces, the womb is no longer a pleasant habitat. Or it may feel too hot, impelling the fetus to look for fresher surroundings. In any case, the fetus had its own mind and acted according to its own volitions. As to the time when it decided that the hour had come to quit the intrauterine environment, the authorities agreed that no set, rigid agenda existed. Chicks hatched from eggs of the same hen do not all come out at the same time. Seeds dropped to the ground at the same time, sometimes in the same furrow, do not always germinate simultaneously. Considering the marked physical disparities among human beings, did it not make sense that the progeny of vigorous parents should mature faster inside the womb and be ready to come out sooner than the offspring of sickly, delicate progenitors? Well into the first half of the present century, it was a widespread belief that premature babies delivered in the seventh month of gestation fared better than those born in the eighth. This misconception reflected the ancient idea that some fetuses engaged in vigorous activity to break loose from the maternal enclosure: some were robust and could escape, others failed in the attempt and were left drained and weakened by the futile exertion. The former emerged on the seventh month and survived; the weak ones, in contrast, too exhausted from the earlier struggle, succumbed in the outside world if they had not completely recuperated. The concept of "premature babies" is a relatively recent one. Well into the last century the term did not exist in the medical literature. Interestingly, the English language word to designate infants suffering from the ill effects of a premature delivery was "weaklings."

Active or passive, the fetus must follow a rigid postural ritual in its emergence to the light. The undeviating protocol specifies a series of postures: now present the head, now bend the neck, now rotate slightly to one side, and so on. Any deviation from this age-old code spells trouble. Those who would assist the mother must be aware of the possible transgressions. Obstetricians and midwives have traditionally studied models of fetuses inside the maternal pelvis, which represent the unborn athwart the womb, head extended, failing to bow, or engaging a foot instead of the crown into the birth canal. Clearly, there is a correct manner of making an entrance into this world, if not one for absconding therefrom. A French scholar, Nicole Belmont, wrote intriguing pages on what may be called the "topography" of human existence: there is, apparently, an *axis of life* which runs from head-to-foot. Accordingly, we are meant to be born "head first." And there is also its reciprocal, the *axis of death,* going from feet-to-head, as recognized in the folklore of many nations. For instance, the American expression "to go out feet first," usually connotes death. To die "with one's boots on" expresses the idea of lethality in foot-polarized terms. Equivalent popular expressions may be found in various parts of the world. To be born "feet first" (technically "in podalic presentation") may thus be accounted dangerous on both obstetric and metaphysical grounds.[17]

I HAVE SEEN THE FUTURE, AND IT IS NOW.

What has happened to conception and birth in our times? The sanguine feel tempted to answer: "They are well, thank you," and add with a complacent smile that they continue taking place today in precisely the same manner as they have taken place since the earliest times of recorded history (as well as before, one might add). This assessment, unfortunately, seems too glib and unperceptive. The truth is, we do not die as we used to, and by inescapable necessity—since birth and death are mere terms of convenience for phenomena not essentially dissimilar—no one is born in the old-fashioned way. The reason is, of course, that no aspect of our lives today is exempt of the ubiquitous control of science and technology.

Technological control, in fact, starts before conception. It used to be that conception seemed a dispensation of Providence, a gift of the heavenly powers. Today, the present comes from the goddess Technology, a man-made yet awesome and implacable deity. Infertile couples can go to specialists to expedite the process. Using a cannula, slothful, enfeebled sperm cells and reticent, unreceptive egg cells are placed in close proximity to each other inside the woman's fallopian tubes. A borrowed trick from matchmakers who contrive to place shy boy and timid girl in secluded propinquity, the expedient often works wonders. It is perhaps no coincidence that the abbreviation GIFT, from "gamete intrafallopian transfer," is used by experts for this fertilization-enhancing technique.

But assisted "reproductive technologies" have achieved a much greater level of sophistication. Ovaries may be induced to shed their egg cells by hormonal stimulation. The expelled egg cells can be retrieved and inseminated artificially by exposing each one to about fifty thousand sperm cells in a culture dish. The fertilized egg is incubated to the two-to eight-cell stage (not quite deserving the name of "embryo" until after implantation, it is at this time referred to as "preembryo"), and transferred to the maternal womb, where it will develop, if all goes well, into a normal baby.

Only a few preembryos are transferred each time. What about the others, those who stay in the culture dish? They are frozen. Maintained in a state of suspended animation for possible future use. But what should be done with them *eventually?* Dear me! The irksome problems posed by the new reproductive technologies have already caused a huge amount of discussion, books, pamphlets, public demonstrations, and so on. To recapitulate all of these here would be as rash as it is impossible. But the central quandary is worth restating. Preembryos are "potential" human beings. That cluster of unspecialized cells, hardly visible to the naked eye, is definitely imbued with the capacity to spawn, given the right conditions, a complete human being, with its full complement of organs and a capacity for sentience and cognition like yours or mine.

Should the culture dish be emptied down the nearest sink without further ado? Some say preembryos deserve, if not a full ceremonial burial, at least less of an offhand manner of disposal. Should they be delivered to scientists, for research use? Mark that some diseases may be cured by growing embryonic cells to replace damaged tissue. Or else, the incredibly abundant and varied growth-promoting factors that embryos normally express could be harnessed to treat patients with burns, unhealed fractures, and other conditions that cause great suffering today. But some say embryos, though not yet sentient, are human; for they could not turn into full-fledged human beings if they were not human already. There-fore embryo research is morally wrong. To dissuade the upholders of this opinion would take the highly hypothetical set of circumstances, almost verging on the fantastic, that speculative thinkers have come up with. Imagine, for instance, an epidemic plague that would kill all fetuses *in utero,* and that could only be checked by developing vaccines or other treatments that rendered embryo research indispensable. The choice would be between immorality and the extinction of the human race. Only the most fanatic fringe would remain obdurate.

Others say that an embryo is not a human being, in the sense that an acorn is not an oak tree; for even allowing that the acorn enfolds all the potentialities to produce an oak tree, it remains an acorn, not a tree. To believe otherwise would be philosophical befuddlement. And since na-ture is notoriously wasteful in her handling of seeds—human as well as vegetable, for many human embryos are normally eliminated before one succeeds in implanting—it follows that he who dumps the culture dish into the sink is acting in perfect accord with nature's ways. In other words, embryo manipulation is morally neutral. But even the most materialist-minded, if honest, must own that the treatment of early human embryos cannot be fully equated to the morally neutral handling of nonhuman "things," "stuff," or "mere meat." In an essay written by Leon Kass, I find the most vivid imagery that I have yet encountered to bring forth the need of clearer definitions. Because of its truculence, Kass introduces his example with apologies to the reader, as I do now in retelling it. Assume someone finds out, by chance, that human pre-embryos—say in the stage of blastocyst, when they look like tiny spherules in no way reminiscent of the human form—are tasty. Would it be all right, considering that manipulations are morally indifferent, for a resourceful entrepreneur to mass-produce them (this being now technically feasible), then to can them, and to market them as a delicacy under the label of "human caviar"?[18]

We are not anywhere near finding the correct solution to these perplexities. What is clear is that we are not conceived as we used to be. It is common knowledge today that the egg cell of a woman, fertilized in the laboratory by the sperm cell of a man, who may be her husband or an anonymous donor, can be made to develop into an embryo inside the uterus of another woman. In a much-publicized recent case, a postmenopausal woman successfully carried the conceptus formed out of her own daughter's egg cell, and thus became simultaneously mother and grandmother to the newborn child. No, we are simply not conceived as we used to be.

Writing from a feminist perspective, Wertz and Wertz have warned that technology is slowly wresting away all control of the generative function from women. No more sense of wonder upon feeling the first stirrings of her unborn child. Long before this happens, she has seen it through the modern ultrasound imaging technique. Tellingly, however, she could not have seen her unborn child by herself: the ultrasound image must be explained to her by the experts, otherwise she can only see uninterpretable gray and black shadows that mean nothing. Wertz and Wertz remark that birth, which used to be a marvelous experience charged with infinite meanings to the mother, a unique life-giving act that could only be depicted metaphorically as "germination" and "ripening fruit," is now defined as a purely technical problem and an inconvenience for the mother. Thus, in an example drawn by these authors, a university hospital advertised with promotional brochures that displayed a smiling couple, beneath which the publicity phrase was: "Let Georgetown do it."[19]

I cannot subscribe to their sweeping condemnation of obstetrical advances. What I see is a dappled picture. The blemishes and dangers of technology are obvious, and much wisdom is needed to check its uncontrolled growth. But its benefits cannot be underestimated without injustice. The ancient manuals of obstetrics and the memoirs of obstetricians of the past paint a grim picture of complicated births. The blood, the sweat, the screams of the patient dominated the scene. The bedchamber, usually overheated, was permeated by the odor of urine, of the "cadaveric" emanations of mortified flesh, and of the woman's vomitus, for vomiting was stubborn, intractable, or deliberately induced to speed up delivery. The husband, the consternated relatives, and the obstetrician moved about with an abject feeling of utter powerlessness. This impotence was only too real, for among various utensils and instruments of the trade, mention is made of a basin for holy water: specific recommendations are made on how to dispose the tools, the patient, and the assistants, reserving a place for the priest during the proceedings. Tacit admission that in most cases the outcome was dire, and that since medical science was helpless to save the bodies of mother and child, efforts had to be made at least to ensure the salvation of their respective souls.

It used to be that pregnancy and gestation were accompanied by a whole train of vexatious and burdensome symptoms in the mother, while the father commiserated, or complacently looked on, inwardly congratulating himself for having escaped the female condition. Occasionally, by that mysterious "sympathy" that the ancients took so seriously and the moderns disregard, the symptoms would be reproduced in the father. But most commonly the morning vomiting, the sensitive nipples, the aching back, and so on, were unavoidable concomitants of motherhood, which it was appointed the father would escape. Even this we would change. I have before me the 1994 commercial catalog of *Childhood Graphics,* a division of WRS Group, Inc., a company in Waco, Texas. On page ten, it advertises the "Empathy Belly," trade name for a weighted canvas vest provided with anterior protrusions to simulate swollen breasts and heavy weights able to imitate the appearance and feel of a pregnant woman's body. Expectant fathers may wear this garment during the pregnancy of their partners, in order to show "appreciation, communication, and supportive behavior." Complete with instructional manual, consent/release forms, and insert weights guaranteed to reproduce the urgent need for urination brought forth by bladder compression, the admirable device sells for a mere $795.00.

This essay began with an examination of ancient ideas on the nature of semen. In a world of institutionalized technology, what happened to semen, the secretion of secretions, the quintessential liquid believed by Pythagoras to contain residues of brain, and by another exalted philosopher to be the very stuff of which the stars are made? It has become a commodity. It is frozen in liquid nitrogen (semen, too, has been put into suspended animation) and so transported across great distances. In some areas of our disconsolate planet, it may be that it is sold for a profit, albeit illegally. There is no loss of inseminating potency even after prolonged freezing. The "animalcules" of the microscopists of yore retain their viability even after fifteen or twenty years. With advances in cryopreservation, it is theoretically possible that future generations will see a child fathered by an individual who had died a century before his child's birth.

There would be much to say about the contemporary vicissitudes of this remarkable liquid, but it seems inopportune to lengthen these pages. Suffice it to say that technology has done a great deal to remove the fear of its procurement. In the thirteenth century, the Dominican friar Thomas de Cantimpré, encyclopedist and author of popular fables, recounted the awful divine punishment meted out to masturbators. One of them, during his sinful self-stimulation, is struck to the ground while exclaiming: "The wrath of God is upon me! The vengeance of God against me!" Death was the right retribution for this sin, but punishment could be doled out in the shape of miraculous transformations. Thus, another sinner, reaching for his male organ, felt in his hands the loathsome writhing of a snake.[20]

Contrast these apocalyptic scenes with the idea that the lay public has about the attitude of a technician in a sperm bank, imagined handing out a test tube to a prospective donor and telling him, "Sir, please give me a sample. The bathroom is two doors down."

NATURE'S LAPSES

You find yourself in an old-fashioned museum of anatomical and pathological specimens. Most likely, you are alone: establishments such as this are usually dusty and desolate nowadays. You turn a corner and discover, locked in a yellow twilight of decaying liquid fixative, the strangest, most extraordinary beings imaginable. Impossible to look at them without a shudder, but mixed with fear there is curiosity, pity, and astonishment. And you cannot ignore them, either. They seem to grab you by the scruff of the neck and tell you: "Look at us." You obey, and your dearest preconceptions crumble. Gender, identity, number, human nature: all these ideas have lost their meaning. Is this creature male or female? Partly one, partly the other, and both at the same time. That other one, is it single or double? Neither one nor the other: single by the trunk, double by the extremities. That one there, human or nonhuman? You hesitate. Perhaps neither one nor the other. But assuredly not a *tertium quid,* not a hybrid of two dissimilar natures. In everyday language, these beings are "monsters." The word does not exist in contemporary medicine, which brands it as pejorative, stigmatizing and redolent of a superstitious bygone era.

The Oxford English Dictionary traces the origin of the word *monster* to the Latin root *monere,* "to warn." Thus, this word seems linked to the ancient idea, already fully shaped in Saint Augustine, that deviant or exceptional beings appear in the world as prophetic signs, as messengers of the wrath of God announcing disasters to come (*City of God* XXI, 8). Another possible derivation remits us to *monstrare,* "to show, to display," because the features of especial beings elicit astonishment and wonder in those who contemplate them, and mixed with these emotions is the desire to exhibit, to *demonstrate* to the rest of the world the uniqueness of the observation.

Some reckon surprise and wonder among the agreeable emotions. But the fascination of monsters is ambivalent; it is the vector that results from the sum of forces of attraction and repulsion. The sight of a profoundly malformed human being fills us with a kind of vertigo that is akin to that provoked by the contemplation of our own death. For these unfortunate beings are the concrete embodiment of the utmost denial: the negative retort to the long-cherished affirmation of the stability and orderliness of nature. They "demonstrate" the existence of an appalling, incomprehensible confusion or, if you will, a demonic principle of evil

that may intrude at any time to work its awful sabotage of nature's delicate plan. The viewer then learns, more or less consciously, his own vulnerability; discovers the flimsy quality of the stuff he is made of; and realizes the immediacy of his own dissolution. He is then filled with that strange voluptuosity alloyed with horror that is always experienced in the anticipation of one's own death: a sort of nauseous languorousness, part cowardly abandonment of responsibilities, part sweet foretaste of a final return to the chaos from which we came.

Narratives have no such strength. Shielded from direct confrontation, we can brook the monstrous. This is why we love to hear, then echo, less than credible reports of prodigious or "monstrous" occurrences. And the greater our fascination, the more prone we shall be to repeat the fantastic tale. The British philosopher David Hume (1711–1776) remarked that when we do not partake of the immediate experience we still find pleasure in the telling, a sort of "relish by rebound." But if we have a stake in the report, as when it reinforces our prejudice or accords with our most cherished beliefs, "at one blow we part with common sense." Hence, a religious fanatic imagines "he sees what has no reality: he may know his narrative to be false, and yet persevere in it with the best intentions in the world, for the sake of promoting so holy a cause. . . ."[1]

The history of teratology is replete with examples of the latter. One is the "monk-calf" and "pope-ass," allegedly found dead and floating in the river Tiber in the year 1523. Seemingly a sample of cheap sensationalism akin to the tabloids of our day, the report was, in effect, a sample of rabid anti-Catholic propaganda at the peak of the religious wars. The calf was said to have been born with inordinately large ears, an enormous tongue protruding from its mouth, and its dorsum covered by hairy, pendulous flaps of skin. The ass was still more striking: its head, appropriately asinine, joined a trunk provided with womanly breasts and abdomen; one of its forelimbs resembled an elephant's trunk, the other ended in a handlike extremity; and the trunk was covered partly by fur and partly by scales.

The monk-calf, or "monk-ox," claimed the pamphleteers, was a concrete, divine indictment of the transgressions of the monastic orders. Its large ears symbolized the futility of auricular confession; its long, hanging tongue was Providence's denunciation of the nonsensical nature of the monks' doctrines, exposed as incoherent babble or "pure tongue"; and the redundant, hair-covered dorsal skin, a divine mocking of the hood in the monks' habit. As to the pope-ass, its head "is an ass's head, which indicates the pope quite well. . . . Its right hand is an elephant's trunk, which signifies the spiritual power of the pope, with which he hits and rends the trembling consciences, like the elephant, who, with his trunk, grasps, tears, and breaks. For can popism be anything other than a bloody immolation of conscience through confession, vows, celibacy, masses, false penitence, the fraud of indulgences, and the superstitious cult of saints? Its left hand, of a man, is the civil power of the pope, denied him by Christ (Luke, 22), but which he arrogated to himself to become the master of kings and princes. The abdomen and chest of a woman [represent] the papal body, namely cardinals, bishops, priests, monkishness, nunneries, the saints and martyrs of the Roman calendar, and this race, this family of lions and pigs of Epicurus, who care for naught but eating, drinking, and wallowing in voluptuousness of all kinds, with one sex or the other. . . ."[2]

For a time, it was mainly the female who was believed instrumental in perturbing Nature's plan. The ancients saw Woman as an eminently excitable being: emotions transmit themselves so readily throughout her entire frame that they spill over, so to speak, to the fetus she harbors in her womb. No wonder that a mere perception, a fantastic dream, a sudden whim, anything that stirred the mother's "passions" could somehow reach the fetus, on whose plastic, inchoate organs the effect was invariably manifested. Well into the sixteenth century, Pierre Boistuau (*ca.* 1515–1566), compiler of "prodigious" occurrences, described a maiden utterly "covered by hair, like a bear," who was shown to Charles IV, emperor and king of Bohemia. It passed for certain that her striking appearance was due to the fortuitous circumstance that her mother had gazed too intently on a painting of Saint John the Baptist clad in a hermit's fur, which hung on the wall at the foot of her bed, at the very instant when the hirsute maiden was conceived.[3] With charming candor, the great Ulysses Aldrovandus (1522–1607), Bolognese precursor of the science of teratology, explained the large number of births of infants of dark olive complexion in Picardy after the Spanish occupation as a result of the strong *visual* impression received by the mothers during the stressful period of the occupation.

A similar explanation was put forth by Benjamin Bablot (1754–1802), French court physician of the ancien régime, for a clinical case detailed in his learned treatise on the power of maternal imagination.[4] A pious woman of Châlons-sur-Marne developed, during pregnancy, a most ardent admiration for the spiritual qualities of the town's bishop. She repeated to whosoever condescended to hear her that she felt a strong desire to be near the saintly man all the time. Her son was born, and "the years developed in the physiognomy of this child that air of nobility and gentle majesty that are so well conjoined in the bishop's face. . . . Monsignor wished to confirm with his own eyes the reality of the phenomenon." The prelate came, saw the child, and was so struck by the resemblance that he was moved to confer all manner of gifts and a generous subsistence allowance on the mother, who, by dint of strong imagination, had managed to transfer to her son the noble facial features of her spiritual paragon. An exemplary instance, no doubt, of the power of mind over matter.

A jealous husband in the extreme of exasperation was less likely to heed fancy theories on the effects of maternal imagination. Conversely, he could believe them firmly, but interpret them to suit his mania. Thus, a man convinced of his wife's infidelity and obsessed with the idea that their son was illegitimate, murdered her despite an obvious physical resemblance between the child and himself. Could it not be, went his reasoning, that the adulterous woman, overcome by guilt and fear of the consequences of her fault, evoked the image of her legal husband at the very instant when she submitted to the culpable embrace and thereby managed to imprint the husband's features on her bastard son? Evidently, the theory of maternal impressions could go this way or that, all depending on which direction the furious winds of passion blew.

A sudden effervescence of the mother's imagination was not the only cause of monstrous births, but surely it was the most potent: a mere recollection, a memory, an insubstantial vision without objective reality sufficed to bring forth the whole train of catastrophic effects. There were, nonetheless, other causes. Ambroise Paré, court physician acknowledged as the most brilliant surgeon of the Renaissance, listed thirteen, of which three—God's wrath, his inscrutable designs (including perhaps playful, divine "sport"), and demonic intervention—were supernatural, while the rest fell entirely within the scope of human agency.[5] Among the latter were such relatively coarse factors as too narrow a uterus, a defective male seed, and that most troubling of sexually deviant behaviors, bestiality.

On January 9, 1826, the great French naturalist Étienne Geoffroy Saint-Hilaire (1772–1844), recognized as the founder of the scientific study of monstrous births, *i.e., teratology* (a term, by the way, which he coined), presented a most remarkable specimen to the consideration of his learned colleagues during a session of the Académie de Sciences in Paris. The "monster" had been discovered in the ancient Egyptian city of Hermopolis during the excavations directed by the archaeologist Passalacqua, and had just arrived in Paris along with numerous other ancient objects that won the enthusiastic admiration of all the savants of the time. Among these objects was a mummified body, near which were found certain items, such as a terra-cotta amulet in the shape of a squatting monkey, which indicated that the ancient Egyptians believed the body had belonged to such an animal; moreover, the mummy had been arrayed in the same squatting posture that was common in Egyptian graphic depictions and statuettes of monkeys.

These facts scarcely seemed remarkable: it is well-known that the Egyptians worshiped animals as sacred beings and took great pains to preserve their bodies after death. Cats, whose death was grievously mourned, were found mummified at Giza; dogs, at Heliopolis; gazelles and ibises in great numbers at many sites in Egypt; and even snakes, beetles, and scorpions were preserved. Two thousand mummified crocodiles were disinterred from the Tebtynis cemetery.[6] An embalmed Egyptian monkey was nothing to be excited about. However, the specimen that attracted the attention of the learned members of the Académie de Sciences on that memorable winter session was larger and more corpulent than the mummies of the many other monkeys that were found in the same gallery. From the start, it was clear that this corpse was different and that its proper study would require all the erudition and keen analytical powers of the eminent naturalist to whom its study was entrusted.

There must have been great expectation when the bandages were undone. The savants then looked in puzzlement, but Geoffroy Saint-Hilaire *père* had no doubts. The body in question was human—and malformed: it was an anencephalic infant.[7] The diagnosis of anencephaly can be made at a glance: the roof of the skull is absent, and the flattened base of the skull is exposed. The brain has not formed, except for, sometimes, part of the midbrain or brain stem, and in its place one finds a very vascular sheet of membranous tissue. The facial features, including the development of the ears, may be secondarily altered. The bony prominences above the eyes (supraciliary arches) are unduly salient. The eyes fit poorly in orbits of diminished size and may resemble, in their protrusion, a toad's. The palate is often cleft. In summary, the Egyptians had been led to believe that a nonhuman creature, a monkey, had been born of woman. But in this, contrary to Western men of later eras, they saw no dishonor. They disagreed pointedly with their Greek contemporaries, whose pride made them believe that only the human form is apt to represent divinity. Apollonius of Tyana, Greek philosopher of the fourth century B.C., argued with an Egyptian priest that only the human shape, as rendered by the great Greek sculptors, was a suitable object of devotion. His opponent countered that it was blasphemous to pretend to conceive of any shape in the deity and that the worship of animals was superior, for it was symbolic and allegorical of the divine omnipotence.[8]

The Egyptian veneration of animals may have degenerated, if we are to believe Herodotus. When he visited Egypt, he witnessed a shocking spectacle: at a public show, a ram copulated with a woman. Victorian translators of Herodotus used to revert to Latin when they came across this scabrous passage (a practice that barred the unschooled in Latin, and therefore most women, from understanding a text that the prudery of the times reserved exclusively to adult men): *hircus cum muliere coiit propalam, quod in ostentationem hominus pervenit*—that is, the he-goat or ram tupped a woman in plain sight of many spectators (Book 2, 45–48). Some scholars believe that this was no isolated incident, and that in the town of Mendes a buck or a ram was kept for this purpose.[9] Rams are sexually insatiable; their ejaculatory activity remains the same after mounting twelve females in succession. Efforts to discourage the male, as by disguising the sexual partner or spraying the female's genitals with repellent odoriferous substances (for this research, believe it or not, has been done[10]), are blissfully ignored: the male continues to mount each new female with undiminished enthusiasm. Bulls, bucks, and rams deserve their reputation in mythology and folklore as lascivious animals and may have represented powerful deities in ancient Egyptian religion. If so, the spectacle witnessed by Herodotus may have been actually a solemn ceremony marked by a tone of reverential fear.

Apart from exotic exceptions of this kind, the crossing and commingling of animal and human bodies has ever provoked horror. Yet human beings are, in many ways, and by inalterable biologic necessity, comparable to animals. When excessive rationalism threatens to remove warmth, affection, and a sense of community from our lives, we yearn for the impulsive, the primitive, and even the irrational: we sigh for *animalism,* a Nietzschean term. But it is with a shudder that we realize how close to the surface lurks the beast within; we hardly need to plumb our depths before we encounter it. Thus, Nietzsche could say that "men are the foremost beasts of prey . . . their ways of deceiving and trampling each other, their screams when in distress and howls of joy when in victory—all this is a continuation of bestiality."[11] In like manner, for the superstitious of yore, pathology was emblematic of animal regression: in the hacking cough of a child with croup, parents heard the cry of a raven; in the stridulous gasping of whooping cough, the braying of an ass. Disease brought forth the bleating of sheep or the bark of yapping dogs from the very throat of human patients. To our day, clinicians speak of coarse and blunted facial features as "leonine," and cannot help but refer to "crablike hands" (Hanhart's syndrome), "bird-headed dwarfism" (Seckel's syndrome), "pigeon breast," and "finlike extremities," to name only some of the many devastations of congenital maldevelopment.

What are we to think today of the birth of a profoundly malformed child? We no longer believe it a premonition of disasters to come, a regression to animality, or a divine punishment for our wrongdoing. We say to ourselves it is "a disease." Mark, however, that it is a disease like no other. The orderly plan of nature, the prescribed regularity of unity, order, and synthesis have been here dastardly undone *before* the creature existed. Disease may be thought of as an obstacle, an obstruction that surges somewhere along life's course, like an unforeseen rocky barrier rearing its mass on a sea route, hitherto navigable, and causing the ship of the body to founder. But chromosomal abnormalities and disturbances in the genetic material are inherited from the parents—at conception. Thus the very vessel on which the being navigates is badly cracked at the hull. In fact, it was never seaworthy: the sufferer never had a chance to embark on a voyage, but sank irrevocably at the start. Or, if another metaphor is preferred, he is wholly immersed, head to toe, in poisonous, dark water, whose turbidity and deadly quality is owed to a fault that lies *upstream,* at the very source, and must therefore contaminate every pasture and kill every creature that chances to contact it. For it is not this organ or that which is vitiated, it is the organization of the organs that went wrong, and therefore every cell is abnormal. Hence the disorder is not like other diseases, in which an adventitious circumstance came to upset a working mechanism, but we can still adumbrate, in the intervals that the confusion lets free, the preexistent, formerly ruling order. No:

here the error and confusion are in the mechanism of construction itself. The patient is condemned to suffer *a priori,* not on account of anything he did, not even because of a misfortune that occurred in his life, but merely for having existed. Such suffering recalls the Sophoclean lamentation, "it were better not to be born." A hollow cry, alas, to which a wit can rejoin: "Yes, but to whom has *that* ever happened?"

No language has words to express the suffering of parents whose child experiences this calamity. The first response to major, crushing tragedy is only numbness. We are stunned. But when the shock's commotion dies out, a formless anger swells within us. Why should such harrowing misery exist at all? Who determined that this ill should afflict us? *Someone* ought to be held responsible. Having witnessed an absurd accident on the street that took the life of a young boy, André Gide commented that, if the Divine Providence causes such occurrences, Providence ought to be considered *sujette à caution,* that is, liable to legal arrest. Whoever is responsible, He, She, or It, stands accused. Let the accused be brought to trial and "show cause," as lawyers say, why they must allow evil in the world.

The legal proceedings were initiated, in fact, very long ago. The wheels of justice, as everyone knows, turn slowly. This trial has lasted several centuries. The lawyers, both for the prosecution and the defense, have been philosophers. A plead for God's defense is called a "theodicy," a term coined by Leibniz in 1710, when he set out to exonerate Providence on a legal technicality, as it were. Kant, also a defender, defined theodicy as "the defense of the highest wisdom of the Author of the world against the charges that reason brings against it on account of the aspects of the world which are not in harmony with its purpose";[12] a definition that reveals, by its ponderousness, that its author was fit to hold his own in the weariest of legal circles.

It is generally known that Leibniz argued that God is not wicked, but a "responsible" Creator who permits only those evils that increase the overall goodness of his creation. Omnipotent, he might have created a world without suffering. But such a world would not have been as excellent as the one we live in, where a logical, indissoluble connection exists, claims Leibniz, between significant good and great evil. Leibniz might have argued that malformed children are a great evil, but they are also the cause of human compassion, self-sacrificing abnegation, scientific research, altruism, and philanthropy—all of which are good and of such weight as to offset the existing evil. In his view, the world fashioned by the Creator suffers a few blemishes here and there but still manages to accommodate an ample surfeit of good and is therefore "the best of all [logically] possible worlds."

Bertrand Russell was among those who spoke for the prosecution. To dramatize his rebuttal of Leibniz's theodicy he imagined a Manichean arguing that our world is the worst of all possible worlds, in which the good serves only as a backdrop to heighten the evil. Thus, Creation could as well be attributed to an evil demiurge as to a beneficent Maker. The demiurge would have seen to it that evil should always outweigh the good and would have created virtuous men *in order that* they be punished unjustly by the wicked. Likewise, he would have brought congenitally malformed, innocent children into his world, that the virtuous be constantly tormented by this blatant injustice. So great an evil is this, that it would make the world much worse than if no compassionate men existed. Both, evil demiurge and beneficent Creator, says Russell after having discredited the defense, are fantastic; but the imaginary Manichean's viewpoint is no more farfetched than Leibniz's.[13]

There is no end to the subtlety and trickery of the barristers along the multisecular trial. Nietzsche, for instance, stunned the audience in the courtroom by declaring that prosecution was moot because God "had already died." Legal action cannot take place when the accused, or the Accused with capital *A*, "died of his pity for man."[14] But despite all the wrangling, legal proceedings being what they are, a verdict is not in sight. Arguments and counterarguments follow each other, and no sooner does one party seem to be gaining the upper hand than the opposing faction interjects an appeal, or by some pettifoggery achieves yet one more postponement or a new trial under different charges.

At first sight, our own age would seem not to care much for the theodicean embroilment. But we are deep into the strife and root for the defense. We profess that it is foolish to wage war against Heaven and repeat, with Carlyle, that "time spent in frantic malediction directed thither might be spent otherwise with more profit."[15] Malformations, we say, are diseases; not lashes from a wrathful God, but a practical problem for us to solve. Illness is de-theologized. This is the newest version of theodicy: a decriminalization of the evil in the world. At any rate, we have come up with a new argument for the defense: dismiss the charges; there is no crime.

Consider now how things really happen in this our pragmatical, rational, and secular or irreligious world. Genetic counseling is almost universally advocated as a method to prevent the birth of a child with serious congenital malformations, a tragedy to which an estimated 3 to 6 percent of all pregnancies are at risk. Concerned parents come to the genetic counselor either before or after having conceived a child. In either case, they expect to be told the causes of malformations, the risk of recurrence when a malformed child has already been born in the family, the possibilities for prenatal detection, the available options, and so on. Even among the highly educated, the expectations are often unreasonably high. This, of course, is no different from what occurs in other areas of contemporary medicine. Thomas Szasz has put it best: "Formerly, when religion was strong and science was weak, men mistook magic for medicine; now, when science is strong and religion weak, men mistake medicine for magic."[16]

A genetic counselor's calling often brings him (or her) against thorny moral dilemmas and will do so more and more as the science of genetics continues to bloom. When the child is not yet conceived, the discussion takes on a surreal hue, reminiscent of medieval disputes on the nature of angels. For ethical principles (a specialized terminology, not always in good English, is already current: "avoidance of harm," "patient autonomy" [*sic*], and the like) are invoked in the name of a patient who does not yet exist; arguments do not revolve around an identifiable subject, but are centered wholly upon a disembodied, purely potential being.[17] As if to further increase the ethereal tenor of the session, counselors avail themselves of abstract terms, frame their utterances in general concepts, and resort to turns of expression that are aloof and unemotional. This is done out of consideration for "patient autonomy," that is, the patient's right to have access to pertinent information, and to make his or her own decisions. The counselor is only a "decision facilitator," not a decision maker.

Inwardly discomposed, supremely anxious, and with the Damoclean sword dangling over their heads by a hair, the concerned parents ask:

"Will our child be normal?"

The counselor replies: "In this part of the world, the risk of having an abnormal birth is 3.5 percent for the general population. We have studied your case and determined that you have a 7 percent risk of this happening to you."

Oh, the power of numbers! The counselor might have said: "Your risk of a mishap is twice that of other persons," but that would have sounded biased, and counseling is supposed to be neutral or "nondirective." Nothing must be said that smacks even remotely of taking sides. Would that everything in life could be expressed numerically! Counseling, and life, would be so much easier . . . But the numerical explanations of the genetic counselors sound to the distressed parents like a meaningless utterance. Which is why the counseled cannot help asking: "What shall we do?"—only to be met with a wall of "nondirective neutrality."

"Do what you think is best for you. This is an entirely personal decision."

"But what do you recommend?"

"I am here only to provide the scientific information. It is for you to decide whether you are willing to take the risks."

"But tell me, doctor, what would you do in our place?"

"My situation cannot be compared to yours. It is impossible for me to assume your entire life's experience. You must come to terms with yourself and assess how much *you* want this child and what risks you are willing to take."

"I really want this child. But I am afraid. Am I making a mistake?"

"If you are comfortable with your decision, it is not a mistake."

"I am afraid, doctor. Tell me, will I regret it later?"

"If you can live with the consequences of your decision, you won't regret it."

Nondirective genetic counseling is perfectly in keeping with respect for the patient's autonomy. But it is not perfect. Many patients are incapable of making appropriate decisions on their own. Charles Bosk, a critic of this medical practice, has remarked that in those cases "patient autonomy" verges on "patient abandonment."[18]

After the birth of an affected child has taken place, genetic counseling becomes an even more delicate process. In the present state of medical advancement, many malformations cannot be predicted; some may be the consequence of a chance occurrence during gestation, not a genetically transmitted flaw. Here, the counselors' mission is to explain that the parents are not to blame; that they have no "bad genes"; that the condition is an accident: a one-in-a-million mishap. But the technical explanations, the probabilistic happenstance, the statistical computations, and the reference to biologic chance: none of these can erase the deep, troubling notion that there must be a reason why disaster struck here and now. For what does it mean to have a 3, 6, or 10 percent risk? At the level of the individual human being, figures lose their power. In real human terms a tragedy either occurs or does not occur. When it happens, it is a hundred percent; when it does not, zero percent. At every vital question, a yawning chasm opens up between science or philosophy and individual human perception. Many unfortunate parents revert to prescientific thinking, fond of invoking divine (or demonic) intervention: it is the way God punishes us for our past mistakes or how Providence tests our endurance.

What choice do they have? Congenital malformations will always exist, because our genetic material is eminently plastic: it is made to undergo mutations and transformations. Congenital disease is the collective price we pay for evolution. Science and technology will always endeavor to minimize the errors, without ever altogether suppressing them. Nevertheless these two will continue to hold before us the vision of a world of perfect bliss, a future world without suffering and anguish. But they require that we place ourselves in their hands with pristine faith, like that of the early Christians, and meekly await the gift of grace. Philosophy for its part, will continue the theodicean trial, always waiting for a verdict that never comes.

Is this to end on a pessimistic note? Perhaps. But consider our plight. Halfway between two darkest nights—the blackness before our births, and the one that shall follow our deaths—we sail for a fleeting moment an uncharted sea, knowing neither whence we came nor whither we are going. We seek sure guidance and are offered instead scientific theories, religious sermons, or philosophical abstractions. We are the sailors; our would-be guides, the cartographers. But what possible relation can there be between us and them? To them, the trip is lines on a map, triangulations and tracings drawn with a compass and mathematical computations. To us, it is the brine blown against our faces, the swelling sails, the creaking deck, the tensed cordage, the furious gale; then, the storm, the shipwreck, the tumult, the cries of despair; and then, the women-and-children-first; and ultimately the abandon-ship and every-one-for-himself! Curiously, this scenario strikes some as funny: Democritus ceaselessly laughed at the spectacle of human affairs. But Heracleitus constantly wept. Both watched the same show; one from above, one from below. The point is, attitude is not only a matter of congenital disposition; it depends on the placement of one's observation post. Contemplative wisdom, claimed Jankelevich,[19] is a problem of optics. Happy those who can raise their seat! And happiest of all those who manage to lift it so high that they see the entire scene, then the theater, and then the theater's dome like a speck amidst the many tiled roofs! For by doing this they can no longer discern the threadbare shabbiness of the costumes, or the smears on the actors' faces as tears run down their cheeks.

PHOTOGRAPHER'S NOTE

The photographs in *Suspended Animation* run parallel to the text but do not serve as literal illustrations. Dr. Gonzalez-Crussi and I independently visited the same museums in Bologna and Madrid and gazed upon the same skulls in the late afternoon on different days. We share a fascination with mummies, skeletal remains, and wax or plaster representations of human pathological conditions.

Dr. Gonzalez-Crussi knows all about the oozing and teeming that occur before human parts are placed in formalin, but as a photographer I prefer to enter the sunlit room once blessed desiccation has prevailed. I am attracted to historical specimens, favoring always patina, mystery, dust. A sense of the uncanny comes from all the transformations and removals: from a person to a corpse, from a corpse to a chunk of preserved flesh under glass or to a classic outline in bone. Especially unnerving are wax models, the most successful of which, supercharged with realistic wrinkles, or with skin of heightened silkiness, seem too translucent as corpses, too personal as anonymous likenesses: inert, yet dead ringers for Experience.

Photography, that most literal of arts, sets it down and spews it forth—the evidence as documented. I use only available daylight and move my subjects into the light. I find that sunlight falling through glass onto a subject refracted through liquid alters the evidence. The resulting blurring and repetition of detail as recorded on film help to dissolve the impression both of flesh and of death, to evoke the soul "at the still point of the turning world. Neither flesh nor fleshless . . ." (T. S. Eliot, "Burnt Norton").

I would like to thank Brother Hugo Saitta of the Casa Santa Convent, Palermo; Dr. Paolo Scarani, founder of the Museum Caesar Taruffi, Istituto di Anatomia e Istologia Patologica, Università di Bologna; Dr. Javier Puerta of the Facultad de Medicina, Universidad Complutense, Madrid; Dr. Juan Francisco Pastor, founder of the Museo Anatómico, Facultad de Medicina, Valladolid; and the staff of the Warren Museum, Harvard University Medical School. Every one of these remarkable curators and custodians treated the enterprise with great helpfulness and even greater kindness. Many grateful thanks also to Agnes Zander who assisted me with infinite patience.

Technical note: The photographs in this book were taken on Fujichrome film with a Nikon FE2, using a 55mm lens and a 105mm macro lens.

NOTES

MICROCOSM IN A BOTTLE

1. Roger E. Stevenson: "Causes of Human Anomalies: An Overview and Historical Perspective" in Roger E. Stevenson, Judith G. Hall, and Richard M. Goodman: *Human Malformations and Related Anomalies* (in 2 vols.). Chapter 1. Oxford Monographs on Medical Genetics. Oxford University Press. New York. 1993. Page 1.

2. Fr. Benito Gerónimo Feijóo: *Theatro crítico universal, o Discursos varios en todo género de materias, para desengaño de errores comunes* (in 8 vols.). Vol. 8. Herederos de Francisco del Hierro. Madrid. 1739. Pages 316–320.

3. Jonathan S. Wigglesworth: "Causes and Classification of Fetal and Perinatal Death" in Jonathan S. Wigglesworth and Don B. Singer (eds.): *Textbook of Fetal and Perinatal Pathology* (in 2 vols.). Chapter 4. Blackwell Scientific Publications. Oxford. 1991. Page 78.

4. Sir Thomas Browne: *Religio Medici*. Part I, section 39. Edited by W. A. Greenhill. Sherwood Sugden & Co. Peru, Illinois. 1990. Page 63.

5. The following sources were consulted concerning disposal of the placenta in different communities throughout the world: John M. Graham, Katherine C. Donahue, and Judith G. Hall: "Human Anomalies and Cultural Practices," chapter 8 in R. E. Stevenson, J. G. Hall, and R. M. Goodman: *Human Malformations and Related Anomalies;* J. R. Davidson: "The Shadow of Life: Psychological Explorations for Placenta Rituals." *Culture, Medicine and Psychiatry* 9: 75–92. March 1985; Maria Leach and Jerome Fried: *Funk and Wagnall's Standard Dictionary of Folklore*. Funk & Wagnall's. New York. 1972. Pages 24–26.

6. J. R. Davidson: "The Shadow of Life."

7. The practice of placentophagy is briefly discussed by Wenda R. Trevathan in *Human Birth: An Evolutionary Perspective*. Aldine de Gruyter. New York. 1987. Pages 104–108. A popular treatment of its contemporary aspects in North America is to be found in K. Janszen: "The Meat of Life." *Science Digest*. Nov./Dec. 1980.

8. Gottfried Wilhelm Leibniz: *Essais de théodicée*. Part 2, 121, VI. Garnier-Flammarion. Paris. 1969. Page 176 (author's translation).

OF FLAYING, DISMEMBERMENT, AND OTHER INCONVENIENCES

1. Ruth Richardson: *Death, Dissection and the Destitute*. Routledge and Kegan. New York. 1987. Pages 35–37.

2. Philippe Grignoux: "Corps osseux et âme osseuse: Essai sur le chamanisme dans l'Iran ancien." *Journal Asiatique* 267: 41–79. 1979.

3. Roger Caillois: *Au coeur du fantastique*. Gallimard. Paris. 1965.

4. Anecdotes concerning the skulls of prominent historical figures are drawn from the interesting work of Folke Henschen: *The Human Skull: A Cultural History,* with an introduction by Kenneth P. Oakley. Translated from the Swedish by Stanley Thomas. Frederick A. Praeger. New York. 1965.

5. Sir Thomas Browne: *Christian Morals,* part III, section 10, in W. A. Greenhill (ed.): *Sir Thomas Browne's* Religio Medici, Letter to a Friend, &c. *and* Christian Morals. Sherwood Sugden & Co. Peru, Illinois. 1990. Page 210.

BOLOGNA, THE LEARNED

1. Mondino de' Liuzzi: *Anothomia*. Pavia. 1478. A facsimile edition of this historical book was published in Ernest Wickersheimer (ed.): *Anatomies de Mondino dei Luzzi et de Guido de Vigevano*. Paris. 1926. The incorporation of anatomy in the curriculum of medical studies at the University of Bologna was largely due to the work of a reformer, Taddeo Aldreotti, and his followers. See Nancy G. Siraisi: *Taddeo Aldreotti and His Pupils: Two Generations of Italian Medical Learning*. Princeton University Press. Princeton. 1981.

2. The myth of a medieval taboo on anatomical dissection has endured for a long time, but it has been reduced to its rightful modest proportion by the scholarship of, among others, Katharine Park and Nancy Siraisi. Park's indictment is that this view, besides being factually inaccurate and distorted, ascribes to the people of a past era sentiments alien to their own and more congruous with our modern sensibilities. This author provides an insightful appreciation of differences in attitude toward the body and its postmortem disposal in Katharine Park: "The Sensitive Corpse: Body and Self in Renaissance Medicine" (Presented at the Interdisciplinary Symposium, "Imaging the Self in Renaissance Italy," at the Gardner Museum, Boston, February 1, 1992). See also Nancy G. Siraisi: *Medieval and Early Renaissance Medicine*. University of Chicago Press. Chicago. 1990.

3. In 1521, a professor of anatomy, Jacopo Berengario da Carpi, boasted, no doubt in a fit of vanity, in his *Commentaries on Mondino,* that he had once given a demonstration in front of 500 students. Quoted by G. Marinotti in "L'insegnamento dell'anatomia in Bologna prima del secolo XIX." *Studi e memorie per la storia de l'università di Bologna* 2: 3–146. 1911.

4. The definitive work on the history of anatomical dissection in the Bologna amphitheater at the Archiginnasio is the scholarly monograph by Giovanna Ferrari: "Public Anatomy Lessons and the Carnival: The Anatomy Theater of Bologna." *Past and Present* 117: 50–106. 1987. I gratefully acknowledge my debt to this important work for much of the historical information in this chapter, as well as the ideas on the psychological significance of the dissectors' task.

5. M. G. Nardi: "Statuti e documenti riflettenti la dissezione anatomica umana e la nomina di alcuni lettori di medicina nell'antico 'studium generale' fiorentino." *Rivista di storia delle scienze mediche e naturali* 47: 237–249. 1956.

6. Robert M. Sapolsky: "Poverty's Remains." *The Sciences.* Pages 8–10. Sept./Oct. 1991.

7. The real cause of SIDS is still unknown. For a recent article on controversy over its definition, see W. G. Guntheroth, P. S. Spiers, and R. L. Naeye: "Redefinition of the Sudden Infant Death Syndrome: The Disadvantages." *Pediatric Pathology* 14: 127–132. 1994.

8. Lodovico Frati: *La vita privata di Bologna dal secolo XIII al XVII.* Bologna. 1900.

9. Ambroise Paré: "Discours de la mumie, de la licorne, des venins et de la peste," in *Oeuvres.* J. F. Malgaine (ed.). Vol. III. Paris. 1841. Pages 482 ff.

10. For interesting and thorough information on Zumbo, with a fine iconography of his work, see Paolo Giansiracusa: "Lettura critica dei 'Teatri della morte' di G. G. Zumbo. Con una nota biografica essenziale e l'inventario del notaio F. Lange" in Paolo Giansiracusa (ed.):

Vanitas vanitatum. Studi della ceroplastica di Gaetano Giulio Zumbo. Arnoldo Lombardi. Siracusa. 1989. Pages 11–42. (A publication of the exhibit in the Regional Gallery of Palazzo Bellomo, Syracuse, Sicily, December 10, 1988, to January 15, 1989.)

11. Élisabeth Vigée-Lebrun: *Souvenirs.* Vol. I. Edited by C. Hermann. Editions des Femmes. Paris. 1984. Pages 237–238.

12. Lesley Dean-Jones: *Women's Bodies in Classical Greek Science.* Clarendon Press. Oxford. 1994. The uterus as "wineskin" is discussed on pages 65–69.

13. Ann Ellis Hanson and David Armstrong: "The Virgin's Voice and Neck: Aeschylus, Agamemnon 245 and Other Texts." *British Institute for Classical Studies* 33: 97–100. 1986.

14. San Isidoro de Sevilla: *Etimologías.* (11.1.77). José Oroz Reta and Manuel Marcos Casquero (eds.). Biblioteca de Autores Cristianos. Madrid. 1983. Quoted by Thomas Laqueur in *Making Sex: Body and Gender from the Greeks to Freud.* Harvard University Press. Cambridge. 1990.

15. Thomas Laqueur: *Making Sex.* Chapter 2, page 37, figure 2.

16. I used the Spanish translation: L. Testut and O. Jacob: *Tratado de anatomía topográfica con aplicaciones médico-quirúrgicas.* 8th ed., vol. 1. Salvat, Mexico. 1952. Pages 644–645.

WAXING PHILOSOPHICAL . . . AND A BIT HYPERSENSITIVE

1. T. Garzoni da Bagnacavallo: *La piazza universale di tutte le professione del mondo.* Venice. 1601. Page 509. Quoted in *Le cere anatomiche bolognesi del settecento.* Publication of *Università degli studi di Bologna. Accademia delle scienze.* Sept.–Nov. 1981. Clueb. Bologna. Page 23.

2. The definitive work on anatomical wax models, likely to remain so for many years to come, is the beautifully illustrated, thoroughly researched, and appealingly written work of Michel Lemire: *Artistes et mortels,* with photos by B. Faye. Chabaud. Paris. 1990. See also Michel Lemire: "Representation of the Human Body: The Colored Wax Anatomic Models of the 18th and 19th Centuries in the Revival of Medical Instruction." *Surgical and Radiologic Anatomy* (Berlin) 14: 283–291. 1992.

3. Lesley Dean-Jones: *Women's Bodies in Classical Greek Science.* Clarendon Press. Oxford. 1994. Pages 69–77.

4. For a scholarly article on intravascular injection methods used by the early anatomists, see the chapter entitled "The History of Anatomical Injections," by F. Cole, in Charles

Singer: *Studies in the History and Method of Science.* Vol. 2. Clarendon Press. Oxford. 1921. Page 207.

5. A description of the bizarre collection of Frederik Ruysch, from which much of the information quoted was taken, is given in A. M. Luyendijk-Elshout: "The Death Enlightened: A Study of Frederik Ruysch." *Journal of the American Medical Association,* vol. 212, no. 1: 121–126. April 6, 1970. Those interested in the technical aspects of his work will find detailed descriptions in Charles Singer (ed.): *Studies in the History and Method of Science.*

6. Giacomo Leopardi: *Dialogo di Federigo Ruysch e delle sue mummie* in *Opere.* Vol. I. Florence. 1969. Page 134. For a more recent edition, see Leopardi's *Operette morali.* 2nd ed. Economica Universale Feltrinelli. Milan. 1993. The mentioned dialogue is on pages 150–155.

7. Giovanna Ferrari: "Public Anatomy Lessons and the Carnival: The Anatomy Theater of Bologna." *Past and Present* 117: 50–106. 1987.

8. Goethe's weakness for anatomical wax models could not have failed to become an object of curiosity for physicians. The medical literature mentions several details of the great man's proclivity in this regard. See J. Scwalbe: "Zur Geschichte der 'plastischen Anatomie.'" *Deutsche med. Wochenschr,* vol. 22, no. 47: 761–763. Nov. 19, 1896. For a more recent reference see Thomas Schwalbe: "Johann Wolfgang von Goethe—ein entschiedener Fursprecher anatomischer Wachsmodelle." *Anatomischer Anzeige (Jena)* 168: 391–394. 1989.

HOW WE COME TO BE

1. Aristotle: *Generation of Animals.* Translated by A. L. Peck. Loeb Classical Library. Cambridge, Mass. 1953.

2. Diogenes Laertius: *Life of Pythagoras.* Translated by R. D. Hicks. Loeb Classical Library. Cambridge, Mass. 1979. Page 28.

3. Aristotle: *Problems.* Translated by W. S. Hett. Loeb Classical Library. Cambridge, Mass. 1970. Pages 108–109.

4. Medical concepts on sexuality during the Middle Ages are well treated in Danielle Jacquart and Claude Thomasset: *Sexualité et savoir medical au moyen age.* Presses Universitaires de France. Paris. 1985. For a general, recent treatise on medical ideas, including those on sexuality, during this historical era, see also Nancy G. Siraisi: *Medieval & Early Renaissance Medicine: An Introduction to Knowledge and Practice.* University of Chicago Press. Chicago. 1990.

5. Galen: *De locis affectis,* book 6, in C. G. Kuehn (ed.): *Claudii Galeni opera omnia.* Vol. 8. Leipzig. 1824. Pages 417–420. See also, in French translation, *Oeuvres anatomiques, physiologiques et médicales de Galien.* Vol. 2. Translated by Charles Daremberg. Paris. 1856. Pages 687–689.

6. Quoted by Jean Stengers and Anne Van Neck in their book *Histoire d'une grande peur: la masturbation.* Université de Bruxelles. Brussels. 1984.

7. Leslie Roberts: "Does Egg Beckon Sperm When the Time Is Right? New Findings Suggest That the Human Egg Sends a Chemical Signal to the Sperm When It Is Ready to Be Fertilized." *Science* 252: 214. April 12, 1991.

8. Danielle Jacquart and Claude Thomasset: *Sexualité et savoir medical.*

9. Jean-Louis Flandrin: *Le sexe et l'occident. Evolution des attitudes et des comportements.* Seuil. Paris. 1981.

10. Jean-Louis Flandrin: "Sex and Married Life in the Early Middle Ages: The Church's Teaching and Behavioral Reality" in Philippe Ariès and André Bejin (eds.): *Western Sexuality: Practice and Precept in Past and Present Times.* Chapter 10. Translated by Anthony Forster. Basil Blackwell. New York. Pages 114–129. For the role of feminine pleasure in sexuality according to the ideas of classical antiquity, see also Lesley Dean-Jones: "The Politics of Pleasure: Female Sexual Appetite in the Hippocratic Corpus" in Donna C. Stanton (ed.): *Western Sexuality: Discourses on Sexuality from Aristotle to AIDS.* The University of Michigan Press. Ann Arbor. 1992. Pages 48–77.

11. François Marie Arouet Voltaire: *Dialogues d'Evhemère. Dialogue IX: Sur la génération* in *Dialogues et anecdotes philosophiques.* Ed. Garnier Frères. Paris. 1966. Pages 442–447.

12. Quoted by Elizabeth P. Gaskins in her book *Investigations into Generation: 1651–1828.* Johns Hopkins. Baltimore. 1967. Pages 52–58.

13. Quoted by Elizabeth P. Gaskins, *Investigations into Generation.*

14. Pierre Darmon: *Le mythe de la procréation a l'age baroque.* Fayard. Paris. 1977. This book is an engrossing compilation of fanciful ideas on conception, pregnancy, and delivery during the seventeenth and eighteenth centuries. Apparently written with an eye for the entertaining and astonishing, nevertheless it constitutes a work of commendable scholarliness. An indispensable reference work on the mentioned period.

15. Jacques-Benigne Bossuet: *Oraison funèbre de Henriette Anne d'Angleterre, Duchesse d'Orléans. Prononcée à Saint-Denis le vingt et unième jour d'août 1670,* in *Oeuvres.* Gallimard, Bibliotheque de la Pléiade. Paris. 1961. Page 85.

16. *Archives Curieuses* (in 27 vols.). Cimber & Danjou. Paris. 1838–1840. See vol. 14, pages 479–480.

17. Nicole Belmont: *Les signes de la naissance. Etude de representations symboliques associées aux naissances singulières.* Plon. Paris. 1971. The major emphasis of this book is dual: anthropological and linguistic. It is thoroughly researched. Those interested in the study of birth will find here the most comprehensive treatment of certain "singular" births, such as infants born in a caul, and many curious facts relating to birth.

18. Leon Kass: "The Meaning of Life—in the Laboratory" in Kenneth D. Alpern (ed.): *The Ethics of Reproductive Technology.* Oxford University Press. Oxford. 1992. Pages 98–116.

19. Richard Wertz and Dorothy Wertz: *Lying-In: A History of Childbirth in America.* Yale University Press. New Haven. 1989. Page 267. Already in its second edition, this thoughtful work surveys the history of obstetrical practice in the United States from colonial times to the present. The authors' viewpoint is feminist. Balanced and illuminating, this book uncovers the risks in the relentless technologization of a crucial human experience. See also Emily Martin: *The Woman in the Body.* Beacon Press. Boston. 1988.

20. Quoted by J. Stengers and A. Van Neck: *Histoire d'une grande peur.* Pages 29–30.

NATURE'S LAPSES

1. David Hume: *On Miracles.* Part II. Open Court. La Salle, Illinois. 1992. Page 36.

2. The famous description of two monsters by Martin Luther and Philip Melanchthon appeared in 1523 under the title *Deuttung der czwo* [ancient Low German form of *zwei*] *grewlichen Figuren, Bapstesels czu Rom und Munchkalbs zu Freyberg ijnn Meijsszen funden* (Interpretation of two monstrous forms, the Pope-ass of Rome and the Monk-ox, found in Freïburg-am-Main). It was promptly translated into other languages, including, of course, Latin: *Interpretatio duorum horribilum monstrorum, Papaselli Romae in Teberi, anno 1493, inventi et monachoviti. Fribergae in Misnia anno 1523, editi per Phiippum Melanchtonem et Martinum Lutherum.* It has been edited in Martin Luther's *Werke* (58 vols.). Vol. XI. Weimar, 1883–1948. Pages 370–385. A large part is rendered into French in John Grand Carteret: *L'histoire, la vie, les moeurs et la curiosité par l'image, le pamphlet et le document.* Vol. 2. Librairie de la Curiosité et des Beaux Arts. Paris. 1927.

3. The idea that the maternal imagination can shape the progeny is traced by Marie Hélène Huet in her scholarly book *Monstrous Imagination* (Harvard University Press.

Cambridge. 1993), to Empedocles, who recommended sculptures and paintings of beautiful subjects to the contemplation of pregnant women. Huet, whose book should be obligatory to students of historical aspects of teratology, also states that the story of the "hairy virgin" was first recounted by Pierre Boaistuau in his work *Histoires prodigieuses,* first published in Paris in 1560. This work has been reprinted by the Club Français du Livre (Paris) in 1961; for the pertinent narrative see page 24.

4. Louis-Nicolas-Benjamin Bablot: *Dissertation sur le pouvoir de l'imagination des femmes enceintes, dans laquelle on passe successivement en revue tous les grands hommes qui, depuis plus de deux mille ans, ont admis l'influence de cette faculté sur le FOETUS, et dans laquelle on répond aux objections de ceux qui combattent cette opinion.* Croullebois & Royez. Paris. 1788. For references and excerpts of the work of Bablot, see Marie Hélène Huet: *Monstrous Imagination,* and the entertaining book of Pierre Darmon: *Le Mythe de la procréation à l'age baroque.* Fayard. Paris. 1977.

5. Ambroise Paré: *Des monstres et prodiges.* First published in Paris in 1573, as part of his *Deux livres de chirurgie.* A critical edition by Jean Céard was published in 1971 (Droz. Geneva); the classification of monstrosities appears on page 4. For an English translation see *On Monsters and Marvels,* translated by Janis L. Pallister. University of Chicago Press. Chicago. 1982. For a superb review of the concepts on monstrosity that prevailed in Europe during the age of Paré, see the scholarly article by Katharine Park and Lorraine J. Daston: "Unnatural Conceptions: The Study of Monsters in Sixteenth and Seventeenth Century France and England." *Past and Present, A Journal of Historical Studies* (Oxford), number 92: pages 20–54. Aug. 1981.

6. Ange-Pierre Leca: *The Cult of the Immortal. Mummies and the Ancient Way of Death.* Translated by Louise Asmal. Granada. Paladin Books. London. 1982.

7. The episode of the correct identification of the mummy as an embalmed anencephalic infant by Saint-Hilaire is recounted by Ernest Martin in his book *Histoire des monstres depuis l'antiquité jusqu'à nos jours.* C. Reinwald et Cie. Paris. 1880.

8. Quoted by William Edward Hartpole Lecky: *History of European Morals: From Augustus to Charlemagne* (in 2 vols.). Longmans, Green & Co. London. 1902.

9. This opinion is expressed by Ernest Martin in *Histoire des monstres,* who quotes Strabo (book VII, 3) and Clement of Alexandria's *Proterptikos,* as well as by Jean Baissac: *Histoire de la religion.* Vol. 2. Paris. 1877. Page 263.

10. For reports on the strong copulatory activity of bulls and rams, see: M. W. Schein and E. B. Hale: "Stimuli Eliciting Sexual Behavior" in F. Beach (ed.): *Sex and Behavior.* John